Love Lets Us Down

A Novel in Stories

by

Suzanne Heagy

To the President!

All Nations Press
Virginia Beach, VA

Praise for *Love Lets Us Down*

"*Love Lets Us Down* is a stunning blend of *Beetlejuice*, *No Exit*, and *Waiting for Godot*. The guests, employees, and ghosts in this 'Hotel California' struggle not only with how to be in tricky relationships, but how to just be.

Heagy's portraits of aloof parents, long-suffering siblings, desperate lovers, ignored children, are carefully and heart-wrenchingly drawn. You will recognize these people. You may be these people. You will root for these people to make it out alive."

—Marie Manilla, Author of *The Patron Saint of Ugly*, *Shrapnel*, and *Still Life with Plums*

"*Love Lets Us Down* presents a drab hotel in the Midwest that becomes an unlikely junction for travelers who at first seem to share only geographical happenstance. They are the forlorn, the lost, those unsure of what they seek, those unaware of what they lack, and even the dead. Suzanne Heagy piles up layers of vignettes of these searchers—all expertly drawn and deserving of novels of their own—to the point at which you think they'll collapse like a Jenga stack, but then the magic begins. With a low-simmer style somewhere between Shirley Jackson's eye for darkness in the corners of our hearts and Marilynne Robinson's ear for dialogue that aches to release it, Heagy has produced a novel that is in turns winding, whimsical, witty, and otherworldly, yet always satisfying."

—Ron Cooper, Author of *The Gospel of the Twin*, *Purple Jesus* and *Hume's Fork*

"Disappearances, affairs, trysts, hauntings: *Love Lets Us Down* features an ensemble cast of characters in a beautiful dark collection of stories. The hotel Meridian plays host to lives in painful transition and sudden crisis. A boy nearly drowns and his father can only muster blame. A fifteen-year-old girl goes missing in the middle of the night. A newlywed bride is intent on having her honeymoon, despite the trip (and her life) being cut short by a terrible accident. Heagy's stories are gripping, moving, and un-put-downable. Love can let us down, after all."

—Phong Nguyen, Author of *Memory Sickness* and *Pages from the Textbook of Alternative History*

"Love might let us down, but Suzanne Heagy's prose never will. She manages to be funny and insightful, acidic and heartfelt, a keen observer of human virtues and faults. Heagy finds life—gritty and real as well as imagined and transcendent—in the overlooked places in the middle of America. Her characters contemplate marriage, fidelity, faith and friendship in a world of scratchy pillows, ghosts, whiskey sours, cigarette ashes hissing in plastic cups, and 'chemically-adulterated water shimmering fluorescent', a world that invokes James Joyce in a Best Western, and where the wing-tips of angels 'flutter like rain'."

—Christi Clancy, NPR and *The New York Times*

Acknowledgements

I thank my parents for raising me in a house of books, shelves at home and library shelves, and all the books that have intersected my reading path, and also my early readers, including Deb Brenegan, Christi Clancy, Ryder Collins, Zeke Jarvis, Oody Petty, and Monica Rausch, and later readers and editors, especially Bob Kunzinger and Donna J. Long.

I dedicate this book to Jim Heagy, my beloved husband who had faith in my writing. —HSH

Cover design: Velicia Jerus Darquenne
Cover art: Fotosearch

ISBN: 978-0-9912721-29
Printed in the USA on acid-free paper.

Contents

⁂ June 17, 1964 ⁂

Dorissa Anne Deatherage Millard hadn't meant to die a virgin. Well, she had and she hadn't. She hadn't meant to die a virgin, only save herself until she was married when the act of intercourse was sanctioned passionately and lawfully. In the spring of 1963, before graduation, she walked into the Navy recruiter's office in downtown Oilton, Oklahoma and signed up for service. The only local boyfriend she'd managed to go out on more than one date with was Ed, who was only interested in wrestling off her underwear. She wasn't interested in that or what it led to: a shack on the edge of town without plumbing, beans and cornbread every other meal, a kid and then another kid; her mother was still having them. She told Ed pointblank not to grope her. Dogs might not know any better, but she expected more of people.

She hadn't planned on meeting a handsome seaman less

than a year after being stationed at Fort Harrison, but Don was a real catch, or he was, before he killed them in a car wreck. He was tall, from Kentucky, blue-eyed and dark-haired; dead on, he reminded her of Elvis. He didn't drink. He went to church. He had money because he worked and saved it. Dorissa was as certain as any bride that's ever lived that she was doing the right thing, overwhelmed by Don's sobriety and tenderness, dizzy, gap mouthed, as if a flock of butterflies flitted in her brain. He had the strength, the restraint, the patience, to make her a better woman than she was. Once when they were naked in his car, he insisted they wait until after they were married to do it, Don, who kissed her mouth so thoroughly.

They left the base chapel in deep dusk beneath a sprinkling of rice thrown by the few gathered witnesses. Once they were on the road, Don pulled Dorissa across the Falcon's bench seat. She pressed her left breast against his chest, kissing and nibbling his neck, feeling his hand squeeze her sanctified thigh as he drove one-handed down the brand-new freeway, an eastern stretch of I-465. "It's like riding on top of the world," she said. "Like we're riding on the Great Wall of China." She breathed in Don's ear and pressed her lips to his cheek. "Can't you go any faster, Seaman Millard?"

The Falcon took the off-ramp at sixty-eight miles per hour, approximately forty above the recommended speed, and failed to curve, instead crashing through the guard rail to flip roof over wheels down a steep embankment. Dorissa was thrown clear, landing with a crack of her neck, while Don lost his lungs to splintered ribs, blood leaking like water spilled from a cup.

Three-quarters-of-a-mile from the exit, news of the accident trickled in with the guests. Those already inside their hotel rooms didn't hear it until the next morning. Some never heard it, remaining preoccupied with atmospheric distractions and noises. The hour, after all, was getting late. It was the new chain hotel's grand-opening. All 144 rooms were reserved, replete with the latest amenities: color TV, free pool with diving board, private phones, and air conditioning.

Those who heard the news expressed regret. One woman even cried, and a man thought of his poor dead father, who hadn't died in a car crash but from a heart attack. The woman, who wore a sun yellow day dress, didn't have a tissue or handkerchief. The man shared his, a monogrammed hanky laundered by his mother, who was out on the town back in Cincinnati to attend opening night of *Viva Las Vegas*.

The woman who cried was from Pittsburgh, where the Rolling Stones played that night, recording a live album at West View Park's Danceland. Fewer people attended the concert than the number who turned out for the release of *Madding Crowd*, at New York's Toho Cinema. It was billed as a "curious little Japanese film," a collage of overlapping human scenes, a haunting but unsatisfying narrative of lives spliced together.

Several guests at the hotel settled in their rooms and watched television, eating food packed in Tupperware from home. A man traveling alone ate at the Shadeland Diner. Forty-three children splashed and dived in the pool after its opening and before its closing. The woman in Room 109 led a prayer meeting for her family because they were missing midweek service at Faith Baptist Church in Fayetteville, Arkansas.

The night clerk at the hotel went into the manager's office and turned on the "Fun in Radio" station. On the local hourly, he listened in about the accident, newlyweds, both formerly of Fort Harrison.

Because he was young and serious, the clerk felt compelled to spread the news. He went back out, but couldn't get a word in edgewise. A man driving in from

Iowa had seen the broken railing. His wife had seen it, too, and three police cars flashing at the site. No, the man behind her said, one of them was County. All of them agreed that the exit was closed, traffic detoured though a construction zone.

The clerk, when he saw his chance, put in, "I heard their name on the radio. Just got married, the Millers."

If the clerk had listened more carefully or studied the hotel register, he would have noticed it was Millard, not Miller, and that the newlyweds had a reservation. But even if he had gotten the name right, Dorissa wouldn't have rested in peace. It was a shame she had worn her best dress to get married in, instead of her Navy-issue uniform. Her good dress could have been her legacy to her little sister back home, a floral sheath with a boxy jacket.

But why was she worrying about a ruined dress when greater things had been lost? Dorissa's spirit broke free and floated above her body in the patch of field beneath the freeway. It wasn't exactly a spirit, and floating wasn't what it did. The last thing she remembered was flying through the air. She woke up feeling like a penny spinning inside a spinning glass ball. The world whirled around in uneven elliptical loops, stars streaking past, the railing of the highway, street lamps unreeling like a movie, shadows moving among sirens and red lights, Don rippling in his dress uniform. Somewhere in the background, mosquitoes buzzed intermittently.

"Don," she screamed, "what have you done?" Their honeymoon night was a bust. Don appeared in natural color, as vivid as if he had been cut out and pasted against two-dimensional air, slightly wind-whipped, rocking back and forth.

"Me? You're the one who said, 'Faster, faster'."

She had, but she didn't even know how to drive. He had been going to teach her. "You made us wait. You made me wait, Don."

"And now you ought to be glad. You died a virgin, you'll go right to heaven. Just wait. The angels will come."

"We're married, and it would have been you, and it wouldn't have been a sin."

"The Lord works in mysterious ways. Would you please stay still? You look like a firefly trapped in a spider web."

She missed her body. She tried to see it, but it kept slipping away toward a looping horizon that veered in all directions. Never again to admire her silhouette in a

Cross-Your-Heart in the mirror or thrill to Don fumbling with its hooks. Never again to climb stairs and feel her calves stretch, or her fingers type one hundred words a minute. What was left of her wasn't even a ghost. She'd seen one once in the old Oilton cemetery, the tall, smoky shape of a man in a uniform that looked English. He whipped across from the fence, disappearing behind a tree. It happened that fast—he was there and then he wasn't—just like her skin that went missing. One of her shoes had been left behind, its heel poking up from the grass. As she spun, the heel deteriorated beneath cycles of sun and rain. Days and nights flashed past, but it didn't matter. What was a minute, a day, a year in eternity? "Do you see that? My shoe is ruined. What will they bury me in?"

"Dust to dust. Think about heaven. Have you seen any angels yet?"

All she saw were horizons slipping away, moving over the edge, rolling waves of grass, the bridge of the highway, Donald's wavering body, still pasted on and blocking her view, distant layers of stars that rolled in unison with phenomena in between, the vaporous clouds, streaming lights all night, the flap of a slow flying bird. Heaven was up and she tried to find it, but up would not stay fixed. She had looked forward so much to staying in a hotel. The brochure showed its different rooms. Their honeymoon suite had a queen-sized bed. She imagined being caught in Don's arms, the holy moment arriving when they would kiss and kiss and finally go all the way. "You keep an eye out for angels. I want to see the hotel." There was no reason she shouldn't. What made the difference? It was better than waiting around in a field.

"Stop right there. A ship only needs one captain, and as your husband, I say stay put."

She couldn't figure how to move, anyway. She concentrated, pulling as tight as a knot of piano wire, straining to move, a lick of inspiration tumbling over and over, the atmosphere growing thicker and heavier. But she didn't have any traction. She couldn't get hold. "I'm free now, Don. Till death do us part."

"Don't go," Don shouted, lassoing her with a rope of thread-like gray made of the shadows of the undersides of clouds.

"No, you don't," she screamed and then the rope caught, creating the necessary resistance. She moved, looped forward, not very far but nevertheless there was movement. It was so surprising, she forgot to pull. Why hadn't she realized? She couldn't move without Don.

Otherwise, it wouldn't be a honeymoon. He appeared on the wavering horizon, steady as a rudder.

"Stop right there, and that's an order. We're not going AWOL from heaven."

She listened and didn't listen, testing her capacities: how hard could she pull without knotting the loops into deeply tangled compression? "I never stayed at a hotel, Don."

"And you're not going to stay in one now." But as long as he held her tight with the thread, she managed to make some progress. The speed Dorissa eventually established was twenty-three-thousandths of an inch per minute, approximately three-and-a-quarter inches a day. The rope that joined them stretched taut like a string weighted at intervals by soaking laundry. Don, flimsy as sheets in the wind, remained difficult to pull till the end. He argued so much, Dorissa sometimes slipped the rope, but then she couldn't move. Then she'd have to scream and shout, "Watch me, I'm getting away," before he'd stop talking about waiting and angels and lasso her again.

The direction of the hotel remained a mystery. She had faith if she pulled, she'd arrive. Seasons changed, snow swirling and clotting, sun baking the street's asphalt seams, floating golden pollen, falling golden leaves, looping through a rolling horizon of waves that extended incrementally on. Only Don remained a flat constant, a papery love in her wake.

It took forty years to reach the hotel, but it was still their honeymoon night. Dorissa dragged Don through a second-floor window. They passed simultaneously through the glass, as even as two points on a line. Once they were in, all bets were off. She dropped the lasso and spun forward, through the sheers, through the heavy drapes. It was all she had imagined: matching bedspreads, a floor lamp, a TV and wall-to-wall carpeting. She looped with happiness and said, "We made it."

Don twirled the rope and tossed it, once, twice, again, but each time it puddled in midair like water. "Stand still, Dorissa. I'm telling you, stand still."

She wasn't moving. For a man as handsome as Don, who hadn't aged a day since he died, she sometimes wondered if he'd learned a thing. She caught the rope when he tossed it and gave a little jerk. "Stop being bossy. It's our honeymoon, sweetheart."

"There is no honeymoon. It's over." He flung the rope with his flimsy arm. "Come on, I need you to get to heaven."

"What do I look like, a bus ticket?"

"I told you, you're nothing but a jumpy, little light."

"And you're a catalogue man out of Sears and Roebuck." If she'd been capable of levitating objects, she would have thrown the television at him in spite of the shadows that moved about the room. What were the shadows? Obviously nothing important. "I saved myself for a man who can't even get to heaven without a virgin."

"And I married a woman with a big mouth. Here," he said, kicking at a chair, one of two arranged at a table. It shifted incrementally. "Why don't you do something useful? Straighten this place up."

"I didn't marry you to be your maid."

His page-of-a-leg shot out and nudged open a dresser drawer. "Shut that, then, why don't you?" He wound up his arm and tossed the rope.

"You're not going to touch the bathroom, Don. Don't even think about it."

"You can have the bathroom, it's all yours."

At last, something they agreed upon. Don kicked over a trashcan.

Front Lobby

I.

The old stucco of the Meridian Inn showed its soot, a sprinkling of black specks of pollution. The only guests parked in the apron lot were those registered for more than one night. The hotel sat lengthwise back from Shadeland Avenue. Between the hotel's parking lot and the street, the sun glinted down on a gravel lot where a restaurant once had stood. A large metal shed built to be a garage remained locked up on the corner. At one time, the hotel had been so new that AAA gave it four stars. Over the years it had changed hands and names several times, been recarpeted, rewired, repooled, repaved, and remodeled in various parts. It was currently owned by an investment group with an address in Dubai. Next door to the hotel was an undeveloped wooded lot, and on the other side a storage warehouse. The street was lined up and down with strip malls, furniture repair shops, second- hand stores, pharmacies, fast food restaurants, convenience stores, and karaoke bars, businesses backing into residential zones of bungalows and middle-aged houses.

On the afternoon that the Millards arrived, Marian Carravejo worked the front desk. The guest standing opposite the counter had reserved a room just that morning. She was fortyish and nervous, fumbling in her purse. She said, "I guaranteed with a credit card, but now I want to pay cash." Her purse, real leather, a fashion statement, was shaped like a binocular case.

Marian said, "No problem," and adjusted the method of payment. The on-line booking service, based on availability and season, had scheduled the discount rate. Marian switched the room from front wing to back wing, Room 248. She scanned a key card and permanently added the room to the Housekeeping Report.

She performed the commands without difficulty, a process she knew better than herself. When the woman handed over three crisp twenty dollar bills, Marian counted out the change, sliding it back across the fake marble counter atop a duplicate receipt. "Sign here, please," she directed, marking the space with an X. "I'll need to see your driver's license." The woman handed it over and scrawled her signature, an initial and a last name.

Marian glanced at the signatures and photograph. "Enjoy your stay. Park around back and go in Door Five. You'll need to use your key card to enter."

The rooms in the back were shabby, but Marian had a feeling that "L. Wentz" wouldn't complain. The woman didn't look like she was in town for a business meeting, family reunion, or sight-seeing trip. It would only take a few minutes to be certain. Guests who didn't like their room usually called right away.

Marian dropped the receipt in the bin. She was the Front Office Manager and it was her job to supervise the guest service employees, particularly the rotation of desk clerks, and in the afternoon, if her housekeeping counterpart left early, the housekeeping staff as well. Right now, two employees were on her mind. Augustus, for one, should have already finished cleaning his assigned rooms, signed out and left the hotel. Last week, he had to be written up when he was caught smoking outside with Maintenance. If Augustus Alvarez, Jr. continued to take unauthorized breaks, his employment at the Meridian would be terminated. Marian wanted to believe he was worth taking a chance on, but she didn't have too much hope.

The second absent employee was the evening shift clerk, Elaine, who was scheduled to arrive at two. Her lateness was more infuriating than worrisome. She hadn't bothered to call in, and she wasn't answering her cell. Until she arrived to tend the front desk, Marian couldn't go check on Augustus unless she wanted to call Maintenance and ask Clyde to cover the desk.

Outside, the entry bay and the half-circle driveway were empty. Inside, the lobby was quiet, its clay-tiled floor sparkling with terra cotta shimmer. Across the wide space where fake plants and couches were arranged, a broad staircase rose to a landing that lent the lobby an element of grace it otherwise would have lacked. It was a square space with a wing attached to each side, a courtyard with a swimming pool sheltered in the middle. High vertical windows to the west flooded the lobby with light, catching the crystals of three ancient chandeliers. The swimming pool, where a guest lounged in a chair, was visible through a panel of windows and double glass doors. Guests often remarked on the staircase and then asked for the elevator, a single carriage that rose up and down, busy during peak hours though there were stairs not only in the lobby but at all remote entrances.

When people were too lazy to take the stairs, Marian didn't know how they existed. She was a tall woman who had been a tall girl who had ducked to diminish her height. It was only with conscious effort and practice that she trained herself to stand shoulders back so that even under duress, her posture remained upright. She wore the navy blazer that was the uniform of the Meridian Inn desk personnel, with low heels and quiet gold earrings. To the casual onlooker, she presented a façade of competence and decisiveness. She looked out at the drive and parking lot again. When the phone rang and broke the silence, she answered almost gratefully, "Meridian Inn. How can I help you?"

The reservation request was for the following week, two double beds, two adults, two children. Marian assigned one of the renovated rooms in the front wing with a view of the swimming pool. She was still on the phone when Elaine rushed in breathless, pulling on her blazer. "I'm so sorry," Elaine began coming around the counter, but Marian frowned and held up her hand.

"That's one room for June twenty-first," she said, and gave the man his confirmation number. Only after she hung up and logged off the computer did she speak to the tardy employee. "So, you decided to come to work?"

The night-shift clerk adjusted her lapels and touched her spiky, henna-streaked hair. She was short with soft shoulders and silver-gray eyes like tadpoles. "I had to go to the DMV. There was a line a mile long."

Marian stepped away from the desk. "We'll talk about it later. Go ahead and log in. There's a problem with housekeeping. I'll be back."

She walked across the lobby and up the stairs to the landing lit with sconces, turning left toward the front wing. The cleaning cart that signaled Augustus' whereabouts was parked at the far end of the corridor by the exit. Marian moved toward it, mentally noting a burnt-out light bulb in a fixture. Augustus was working against housekeeping protocol, which clearly stated that the rooms in this wing be cleaned in descending order. As she drew near, she could see and hear that the door to 233 was open, a low murmur of voices switching to the blared music of a commercial. The TV and carpet muffled her footsteps.

Augustus sat on the nearest bed, arms hugging his body, legs crossed at the ankles. The top mattress of the other bed leaned vertical and naked next to the window and air conditioning unit. He turned his head and nodded.

"Hey. What's up?"

He looked so young, his body lean, even the unshaved stubble on his chin. She said, "The question is, what are you doing? You should be finished by now."

He shrugged and pointed to the mattress. "Somebody pissed the bed."

"Where? I don't see it."

"On the other side. I used the cleaner and leaned it up to dry."

Otherwise, the room was neat, polished, adequately arranged. She gingerly touched the mattress and saw the drying edges of an antiseptic stain. "Why didn't you call and report the problem?"

He shrugged, watching television. "The phone's not working."

The pastel-striped drapes and sheers were open. She could see across the courtyard. Down at the pool, the aquamarine water shimmered. The lone sunbather was still there. Half the umbrellas remained unopened.

She picked up the phone and checked it. The problem, Marian discovered, was that it had been unplugged, though Augustus could have used a phone in another room, or investigated himself; it took her three seconds to discover the dangling cord and empty jack. She entertained the suspicion that he had disconnected it, but why would he? Then again, why would anyone? A hotel provoked the inexplicable in people, oftentimes for the worse, rules broken, cheating husbands, cheating wives, people stealing light bulbs, toilet paper, filling nightstand drawers with garbage, burning holes in the carpet or drapes, vomiting, leaving mysterious streaks, even blood, on the bed sheets or the towels. If real damage occurred—stripped fixtures or wallpaper, broken furniture, an actual fire—the owners' lawyers set a claim into motion, a demand for reparations. Marian had been involved in more than one case, a process she particularly disliked, caught between vandalism and hotel lawyers. She hated going to court, the metal detectors, armed guards, the wooden benches and sideways glances. She wasn't the one who tore up hotel rooms, but the courthouse still felt like punishment.

She plugged in the phone and checked for a dial tone. "Next time look at the jack. Did you think of calling from another room?"

"Della said I can't go back in after I finish." He pointed to the TV. "Did you see that? A man cut off his own arm to escape from a landslide."

She couldn't tell if Augustus was actually unconcerned

or ignoring the situation, but either way, his shift was over. "Okay. Let's go. You can finish in here tomorrow." Back at the desk, she'd block the room, remove it from the rotation.

"That's chill," he said, clicking off the TV, dropping the remote on the dresser. He stood and stretched, his hands behind his neck, his arms two angles of muscle. His twisted torso, his sagging pants, moved an angry spin in her stomach. He was just like her brother and all his worthless friends, punks who had no respect for anyone. She said sternly, "I've told you before. You should address me by my name."

"Sure, Marian, it's chill."

His grinning compliance made nothing better. She followed him from the room and shut the door. She instructed him to change the light bulb, and then store his cart and sign out. He was an employee, a subordinate, nothing more. Although she was only twenty-nine, she was familiar with how charm played, like a coiled snake that hides in the grass waiting to spring. Augustus Alvarez, Jr. had had his warning. If she had to, she would fire him.

She walked back toward the front desk, stopping when she reached the landing. The terra cotta space of the vaulted lobby had grown animated in her absence. At the desk, Elaine assisted a man with a wavy thatch of light hair, the likely father of a little boy who was prowling the lobby on his own. Two other children waiting were attached to an obvious mother and father. Maybe Elaine had tardiness problems, but she excelled at customer service, more patient than Marian, less likely to ruffle when pressed by a rush crowd or rudeness. A gray-haired, heavy-set man perched on a wing chair, also waiting his turn. The boy wandering the lobby, maybe three or four, wore a white t-shirt and red shorts. He climbed up on a couch and began to jump up and down, stomping his shoes on the patterned cushions.

Descending, Marian walked toward him, but then a woman appeared, exiting the short hall where the lobby restrooms were located. "Stan," she called in the hushed voice of a conspirator. "Stan, honey, come here."

The boy stopped, climbed off the sofa and approached the woman immediately. Marian continued to the desk, relieved. She still had reports to attend to before a twelve-hour shift released her. She stopped to empty the receipt bin while Elaine passed the current guest his key cards. "I'll be in the office. Come see me when there's a break." It would be Elaine's third warning for tardiness.

The manager's office was behind the front desk and looked to the back of the hotel through picture windows streaked by dust and spotted by rain. A rising bluff of wild plants and stunted trees grew beneath I-465. With the lights off, the office was calm and quiet, a retreat into gray contemplation. Marian could see the traffic streaming past, but she knew they couldn't see her. She took off her jacket and sat down at the far desk that wasn't against a wall. She had two e-mail messages, both general announcements, which she scanned feeling lonely and relieved: nothing had changed, no urgent news or directives. The hotel was above sixty percent booked, with several guaranteed late arrivals. She blocked out Room 233 and readjusted the room report.

Silence floated in the office, the only sound the clicking of the keyboard. After the daily reports updated, she should phone and check on Jared. If she waited until the weekend, her brother might not be around. Every fourth day, he had to leave their grandmother's subsidized housing to sleep somewhere else, or their poor grandmother would lose her one-bedroom apartment. Unauthorized residents weren't allowed; the unit manager was keeping an eye out.

Marian offered Jared the couch in her apartment,

but her brother wouldn't take it, a fact she didn't dwell on too deeply. Whether he lived with her or not, he remained a constant worry. Often when she saw him, he seemed so clear-eyed that what she imagined he did—drunkenness, drug deals, thieving, fighting—disappeared in the optimistic spell cast by his willingness to sit down at their mother's table for dinner. She no longer knew who her brother was. Once he showed up back up at their grandmother's with a burned neck. He said it was an accident with fireworks, but she had a feeling an enemy branded him on purpose.

Marian took out her cell to call their grandmother's house. As usual, Grandma Helen wasn't feeling well. She was down in her back again. Marian listened and then asked to speak to Jared, but their grandmother said he wasn't at home. "I don't know where he goes off to. He left last night and hasn't come back. The phone rings for him all the time. I can't even sit down."

Last winter, Jared went to jail for driving under the influence and possession, freezing to death in a thin orange cotton jumpsuit, no underwear, bologna twice a day on mustard bread, sharing a putrid, public toilet with five other men in a cell with concrete beds. It wasn't the first time he'd been in trouble, but the first time he'd been in jail. Marian suffered for his imprisonment, their grandmother suffered, everyone in the family suffered. Together, they'd managed to raise bail.

"What about his friends? Have you seen Damon?"

"No, and the ones on the phone never say their name. Last night the doorbell rang and when I opened the door, there was nobody on the porch."

"Mimi, don't answer the door unless it's someone you know."

"It wasn't someone, it was no one. I turned on the porch light first."

"I'm coming to see you on my way home. Do you need anything at the store?"

When they said their goodbyes and hung up, Marian turned again to hotel management details, but she couldn't concentrate. Her mind set down a revolving track she could only recognize as obsessive: worrying over Jared was driving her crazy. Why couldn't he be where he was supposed to be, doing what he was supposed to be doing? She didn't care about losing the bail money, only the trouble Jared would cause himself: a warrant, arrest, another fine or worse. She knew he didn't want to go to court. He seemed to have prison wishes. She could hear the clank of cell doors closing. How could her little brother want that?

II.

When Marian went into the office, Elaine breathed a sigh of relief. Her boss was uptight on a good day, but lately she had been disturbed, snapping over nothing, completely bent. So, Elaine had been late, yes, and time was important, but clocks were only objects, and their numbers not only socially constructed, but also arbitrary. The obvious family stepped up to the desk. Elaine nodded once and smiled. "Welcome to the Meridian Inn. How can I help you?"

"We have a reservation." The man, shiny-faced, straining the waist of khaki shorts belted beneath a bright blue polo, pulled out a business card with the confirmation number scrawled on its back. "We're the Sweeneys. We came to town because we heard the international world's fair is in Indianapolis."

"Oh, stop it," the mother said, not maliciously. She addressed Elaine directly. "Ignore Bob, he's always making jokes. We're in town for a convention."

"What kind of convention?" Elaine found the reservation, Room 108.

"Specialty hardware. Bob works for Build-it in

Knoxville."

Elaine waited for the confirmation to print. She had seen a million kids come through, but the Sweeney girl was special. She had ragged blonde hair, a winsome smile, the self-possession of an indy rock star. "Are you going to the convention?"

Blonde hair whipped back and forth. "I'm going swimming."

"She can't go to the convention, she's a girl." The boy, about eight, was plump like his father with his mother's wide-set eyes. "I get to go with my Dad."

"You're going on Saturday," the mother said. "Tomorrow is the Children's Museum."

The blonde girl paid no attention. She picked seriously at a chipped pink fingernail. Elaine confirmed the method of payment and printed the receipt. Bob Sweeney handed over his driver's license and signed. He asked, "What would you recommend around here as far as something decent to eat?"

The gray-haired man, who had been waiting perched on the edge of his chair, lifted himself stiffly. Elaine said, "There's pizza to the right and seafood to the left. Either one is good."

"Pizza," the boy shouted. "I want pizza."

"He always wants pizza." Mrs. Sweeney shook her head. "You'd think his middle name was pepperoni."

The old man hobbled more than walked toward the desk. His right foot slapped the floor with each step and he didn't look happy. Elaine handed Bob Sweeney two key cards. "Drive to the end and go in Door Two. Enjoy your stay."

"We will," said the mother. "This is like a vacation. I needed to get away." She seemed to want to say something more, but the old man wasn't having it. He walked straight up to the counter and leaned on it with psoriatic forearms.

"If you need anything, give us a call." Elaine waved the family good-bye, turning and flashing Mr. Cranky her most winning smile. "And how can I help you?"

"I need a first floor room, no smoking, as far from the pool as it gets, and I want the senior citizen's rate, kid." He had the kind of eyes that demanded contact, a straight forward gaze of pale blue, ice water pools in the splotchy wrinkles of a face set off by a frosty corona of eyebrows.

He was the second guest already to request a room far from the pool, though the Peterson party had specifically wanted a room next to an exit. Some days everybody wanted something special, end rooms or close rooms or far rooms, two doubles or all king-sized beds. Mr. Cranky looked like a front wing guest. "Let me see. I have it. How does Room 112 sound?"

"It sounds old, kid, like me." He waggled his eyebrows up and down.

The phone rang, and she said, "Excuse me," answering, "Meridian Inn."

"Hey, honey bun, can I take your clothes off?"

"Hold, please." Elaine waited the call, masking her irritation. Karen knew better than to say things like that. One of them had to make a living. "Yes, we have Room 112. How many nights are you staying?"

"One'll do it. That the boyfriend?"

"Just a reservation, unfortunately." She didn't care enough to care about his nosiness. He was an old man, almost dead on his feet; pity made him easy to tolerate. "I'll need to see your driver's license. And how would you like to pay?" Karen was the one who should have known better. The light stayed flashing red.

"I'm writing a check. You still take checks?"

"We do, with a second I.D. and verification." His check would be good; Horace Benford's check would be as good as gold, like his silver MasterCard with eternity for its expiration date. She entered him into the system and ran the check through. She printed the receipt, ignoring the old man's tremor when he signed his name. He said, "You have a good day now," and she said, "You, too," wondering that the state allowed him to drive; his license said he was eighty-two.

She turned her back and busied herself with shuffling papers until he foot-slapped out the doors. Alone at last, she looked at the phone. Karen hadn't hung up. Karen, beautiful Karen, the sweet dimples above her hips. Elaine could ignore the call, leave her girlfriend hanging, and knock on Marian's door to listen to a lecture on lateness, or she could pick up the phone and talk.

When she picked it up, she whispered furiously, "I told you not to call here and say things like that."

"Why did you have to leave, Laney? Tell them you're sick and come home. I miss you. You work too many nights."

If only it were that easy. The empty lobby was a bright vacant space, not even the silk palm leaves stirring. A door slammed somewhere far away. "I'll be home by eleven, no later than eleven-thirty."

"What am I supposed to do while you're not here?"

She could get up, wash her hair, go to the grocery store for cereal and milk, scrub the sticky linoleum of the kitchen floor, do laundry—they were down to hand towels—but she wouldn't, so why bother mentioning any of it? "Why don't you watch TV?"

"There's nothing on. It's depressing. I think I want to go out."

She didn't have any money. Someone else would buy her wine. Maybe if Karen would get a job, but Elaine didn't want to bring it up. A maroon mini-van drove into the entry bay. The color was a flash of inspiration. Elaine said, "What about the boxes? Go through them and see what you find."

"You told me not to open them."

They contained the material remains of Elaine's mother's aunt, boxes due to be shipped to Florida as soon as Elaine could afford it. In the meantime, possession was ninety-nine percent of the law. "Go ahead. It's okay."

"Do you think the red dress is in them?"

"I don't know, maybe." Four girls and two women unloaded from the van, stretching and walking around. "I have to go. Stay home, okay? Promise me you'll stay home."

But Karen wouldn't promise, only said, "I love love you," before she disconnected. The girls lounged outside in the entry bay's shade. The two women pushed through the doors.

III.

At five o'clock sharp, Duncan rounded into the lobby, loaded with his thermos, a canvas satchel, and a paper sack in which was carefully packed his lunch. Weaving his way around two guests talking, he pushed behind the desk, setting the thermos on the counter and straightening his tie, adjusting the cuffs of his blazer.

Elaine looked up from her computer. "Hello, Duncan. How are we today?"

"I'm fine, I don't know about you." With the toe of his large black work shoe, he nudged the satchel under the lower desk.

"At least you finally showed up. Now you can deal with Marian."

"What did you do this time?" Duncan logged on to the second station. He watched as three girls raced down the stairs, followed by a teenager descending alone. She had a towel wrapped around like a terry cloth sarong, one delicate hand following the banister. In five or six years, she might be okay but for now she was nothing but jail-bait.

"So, I was late, like twenty minutes. That doesn't mean I'm the problem."

The girls proceeded out to the pool. Whatever went on between Elaine and their boss, Duncan had no intention of getting in the middle, though he was certain as the Little Ice Age that, regardless of the circumstances, he'd align himself with Marian. When he was in training, she'd once said, "The best advice I can give you is to always pay attention," which at that moment had seemed profound, so serious were her almond shaped, rootbeer-colored eyes. From the day he was hired, he'd felt it; she was a different species of woman, not like his one-and-only psycho ex-girlfriend, who after a night out with "the girls," came in and told him to follow her to the kitchen, where she laid out a cutting board, threw a condom down on it, and stabbed it with a butcher knife. "That," she said, "is what will happen to you if you ever mess around on me."

Marian would never descend into barbarism, threatening a man with castration. In the year that Duncan had worked at the hotel, he'd discovered nothing uncivilized about her: her favorite food was Italian, sometimes Thai; she wore a size seven-and-a-half shoe; her favorite movie was *The Wizard of Oz*; the first time she voted was for Ross Perot, and when he asked her why, she said, “I wanted change,” a reasonably progressive answer. She didn’t have a boyfriend or at least had never mentioned one. She didn’t seem to get personal calls, though she did have family in the area. Someday when he felt lucky, he planned to ask her out, something innocent to start with like miniature golf or bowling.

“If you don’t believe she’s in a bad mood, go find out yourself.” Elaine nodded toward the manager’s office door.

Which he had intended to do, anyway. Duncan picked up his thermos and lunch sack and sauntered into the office.

Marian, as beautiful as ever, looked up with effervescent eyes, her olive cheeks dappled with freckles. “Hey,” he said, “how’s it going?”

“I’m almost finished. Just hold on.” She did seem somewhat distracted. She typed one last thing and then started shutting down. “We’re sixty percent booked, with six rooms out of circulation. Do you have any questions?”

Although he answered, “None that I can think of,” he did have at least one. “Is everything okay? Did Elaine do something?”

"No," she said. "She was late, but I'll take care of it tomorrow. I have some personal business today."

He would have liked to inquire further, but he feared stepping over the line. When he broke up with his ex for stabbing a condom, she'd said, "Don't think it's a tragedy, Duncan. I can always do better," and, despite the fact that she was excessively violent, he had to acknowledge she might be right. His ex had a sense of humor, an accounting degree, and was a natural blonde. He, on the other, packed a near-spare tire and was eleven credits short of a BA in History. He earned little more than subsistence wages slaving at a mid-rate hotel. He often forgot to have his oil changed. His toothbrush was always worn out. "I hope it's not your grandmother. If it is, tell her Duncan said, 'Get well soon'."

"No, but thanks for asking." She stood and put on her blazer. "I'm stopping by to see her. I'll tell her Duncan said hi."

When she stretched to slip her arms into the sleeves, her button-front blouse flashed open, allowing a glimpse of a flesh-colored bra minus ornamentation. Not only was Marian his emotional type—calm, competent, minus the drama—but she had a rack that could launch a world war if the world would ever stop having one. He followed her out of the office, saying, “Don’t worry about a thing. Go take care of business.”

“Go take care of business,” Elaine mouthed once Marian was out of earshot. “You know you want her.”

“No, that would be you.” An inside line rang, Room 157. Duncan answered, “Front desk. How can I help you?”

Room 205

The maroon minivan pulled forward and parked in the closest spot along the apron sidewalk that circled the Meridian Inn. Merry Mentweather, who was sitting in the middle bench seat, thanked God they had stopped for the night. Of course, she still loved her niece Cara, and the girls loved their cousin, her sister's only child. But riding in a van with the fifteen-year-old, being trapped in a vehicle designated "mini" from Pittsburgh to Indianapolis, was taking its toll on them all. Cara had terrorized poor little Julie, said if the girl touched her, she'd scream, and Merry felt so sorry for her youngest daughter that she traded to give Cara the front seat, in spite of the fact that Merry got car sick. Her older daughters, Jessica and Janet, napped on the back bench, cuddled up with their pillows. Julie had nothing to lean against; she was closest to the van's door. All Merry's daughters were named Js after their father. She was thankful there hadn't been any boys.

The girls, Merry's girls, looked forward to the trip and especially looked forward to swimming, so Genevieve, Merry's older sister, requested a room near the pool. No reservation; they hadn't planned their stops. They were women being spontaneous. The Meridian Inn had a sign on the freeway, a half-of-a-billboard with an aerial view, a painting, not a photograph, advertising discount rates.

The closest available room to the pool was on the second floor. Genevieve paid with her debit card. The clerk recommended the lobby entrance. Cara threw a fit because she didn't want to carry her suitcase in public. Her Aunt Merry pointed out that the lobby was almost empty, but Genevieve acted like it was a joke, laughed and said, "A princess will be a princess," and carried her daughter's suitcase for her. A daughter should have more respect than to treat her mother like a servant. Merry always told her girls, "I'm your mother, respect me." When they tried her patience, she glared them down and said, "You should do what you're told."

Because the trip was at Genevieve's expense, they had agreed to share one room for the night. When Merry walked into Room 205, her mood improved immeasurably. It was nice and clean, decorated in peaches and greens, large with two queen-sized beds. The pool area was just below them. A woman sunbathed, her back to the sky. The girls weren't hungry; they'd been snacking all day. All they wanted was to swim. It was agreed that Cara would chaperone while Merry watched from the window, sitting at the table with her swollen ankles propped up.

"Now that that's settled," Genevieve announced, "I'm ready for a cocktail." She fished a pint of whiskey from her luggage. "Want one, little sister?" She dangled the bottle.

"You know I don't." Genevieve was the wild one, the instigator in the family. They were traveling to finalize her second divorce, both times from men with money.

Cara, who hadn't wanted to wait a turn changing in the bathroom, stepped out of the recessed closet wearing the tiniest bikini, aqua spotted with bright red strawberries. She threw her clothes in a pile in the corner and struck a precocious pose. "Mother, did you pack my beach towel?"

"It's in my suitcase. There wasn't room in yours."

Merry waited until the girls left the room. She looked at Genevieve, ensconced on the nearest bed, reclined against all the pillows, sipping her cocktail from a cheap hotel glass like it was Austrian crystal. "Don't you think Cara's swimsuit is a little skimpy?"

"She looks good in it, what can I say?"

"It's not how she looks, it's how men will look at her."

"Are there men down by the pool? Maybe I should have gone swimming."

The girls, led by Merry's youngest, emerged from the building and claimed a block of loungers, throwing down their towels and kicking off their flip-flops. Cara looked up at the window. Merry nodded and waved. "I thought you were finished forever with men. That's what you told me last night." Her niece had been an elfish toddler with flyaway, fairy-dust hair. Now the young woman turned without waving back and sat at the edge of the pool, cupping water to run down her arms, wetting her naked stomach.

"Last night was last night. Today's a new day." Genevieve sat up and freshened her drink from the whiskey and soda on the night stand. "What kind of man should I look for next? Young and hot like Demi Moore? Or love, like Candice Bergen."

"I don't know why you keep bothering with husbands." If anything ever happened to Jimmy, Merry's husband of fourteen years, she'd never marry again. She had her children. Men were not her equals exactly. They were hairy beings who demanded their own way, a means to an end, as much trouble as money, at least Jimmy turned out to be. She hadn't thought that marriage would be like it was, but she would never get a divorce. It was against her religion, she'd taken vows: until death do us part. It was what their mother said, and their grandmother too. Men had uncontrollable urges. She worried for her daughters. No men at the pool. In the end, that didn't mean anything.

"I like men. I like the fact they have parts that I don't."

"You're bad," Merry said, half-seriously. "I can't believe you're my sister."

"Believe it, sister. Am I that bad?"

Maybe it was Genevieve's insecurities that had kept her so open, irresponsible, youthful. Of course, she'd only had one baby compared to Merry's three. And she ate more salad, and weird things like hummus and sushi, food that looked calorie-free. "Sometimes you're bad. I don't know if you're crazy or just adventurous."

"Right, I'm so adventurous, spending the night in Indiana nowhere with my kid sister and a bunch of kids.

If we didn't have to drive tomorrow, I'd go crazy and go out. I'm sure there's a bar around here."

Merry's girls splashed and laughed; it looked like they were playing Marco Polo. Genevieve's daughter sat in a lounger drawn beneath an umbrella's shade. "I don't think that would make Cara happy. She's had an attitude all day."

"She's fifteen; she's going through a stage. Just ignore her and she'll get over it."

It was hard to ignore the girl's demands, her rudeness. She set a bad example. "You're her mother. Make her carry her own suitcase now and then."

"I like to choose my battles. A suitcase isn't it." Genevieve sipped her drink. "Let's talk about something else. Tell me again what you want to do in St. Louis."

"You used to live there, you tell me." It was like her sister to change the subject. The girls were having a good time. More people arrived, a family with two boys and girl, who settled on the opposite side of the pool. The man spread the woman's towel on a chair, a thoughtful gesture to Merry's way of thinking. One of the boys was talking to Janet. He looked about ten years old.

"I don't know the facts like you do. I only lived there, I wasn't a tourist."

"What's on TV? Have you checked the schedule?" The room was orderly and clean, soothing, unlike the chaos of home. Merry was on vacation. She was tired of driving, striving, worrying, planning, working, working, and thinking. She rolled her neck and pointed her toes, admiring the scratchy newness of the chair. Genevieve's problems were not her problems. Everything would be fine.

When the girls eventually came in from swimming, they were starving and shivering, chilled by the air conditioning, dripping from the pool. They took quick, hot showers and dressed to go out to dinner. Merry's girls would have been happy with fast food, but Genevieve said, "I need silverware and cloth napkins," and they ended up at an Italian restaurant. It was actually good; the girls all ordered spaghetti. They didn't make pasta at home very often because Jimmy liked meat-and-potatoes. Cara was quiet, Merry would have said sulky, but at least she didn't cause any trouble.

When they got back to the hotel, it was dark and all the close parking spots were taken. Merry, who was driving, backed into a well-lit space in a direct line with the lobby entrance. This time the girls carried in their pillows and blankets, Cara again refusing to help. She said she wasn't carrying anything because she didn't need her blanket or pillow. She crossed her arms and looked toward the freeway where the bright red of taillights appeared.

In the room, Genevieve closed the curtains. In spite of the clothing and toiletries scattered across its surfaces, the room felt spacious and homey, and the air conditioner hummed along. Julie cried because she couldn't find her toothbrush, and then Jessica's stomach hurt, and by that time Merry thought the sleeping arrangements were settled: she and her girls would have one bed and a pallet on the floor; Genevieve and Cara would share the other bed. Her niece had been camped by the nightstand for a while, polishing her toenails, even offering to share the polish with the girls. When Genevieve complained that all the ice had melted, Cara volunteered to get more. Her hair was still fairy-dust brown with golden strands shining in it. She looked so young and vulnerable in her pink shorts and powder blue t-shirt.

"Down the hall to the left," Genevieve called as her daughter walked out of the room. "You know," she spoke indifferently to Merry, "Cara says she's not sleeping with me."

Jessica and Janet watched the movie of the week.

Julie was in bathroom, borrowing her mother's toothbrush. "Where does she say she's sleeping then? There aren't enough blankets for another pallet."

"She says she's going to sleep in the van."

"Absolutely not. That's ridiculous. Right by an interstate in a strange city. Of course, you're not going to let her."

"What she wants is her own room, but I said no. She knew it from the beginning. What she really wanted was to stay in St. Louis." Genevieve brushed her hair behind her ears. She still had her earrings on. "I don't know what she wants, and neither does she. I hope she figures it out soon."

That Genevieve would have a moment of indecisiveness when it came to such a ludicrous request on the part of a fifteen-year-old whose taste ran to handkerchief bikinis was beyond Merry's understanding. "Some things you don't figure out, some things you have to be told. Do you want me to say something to her?"

"No, no, it's not worth it." Genevieve yawned. "Maybe she'll forget about it. God, I need a sleeping pill. Is the bathroom empty yet?"

"Go ahead. I'll get us all tucked in."

When the hallway door opened, all the lights were

turned off except the entry fixture and the flash of the TV. Cara came in and stopped at the foot of the pallet without speaking, waiting until the girls moved their feet before she proceeded to set the ice on the dresser. "Good-night," Merry said. "Do you need another pillow? I have an extra one here."

"I'm fine," Cara said, sitting down on the bed, watching and not watching the movie. She had Genevieve's profile, except for her nose which was more aquiline, resembling her father's.

"Did you lock the door?"

Cara shook her head. She didn't take her sandals off.

"Why don't you lie down?"

"My mother said I could sleep in the van. I'm waiting to say good-night."

It was too bad they weren't any closer, that Cara had grown up so far away, but in the end, it didn't matter: Merry was still an adult and a blood relation. "That's not a good idea. Your mother—"

"My mother already said I could."

"Your mother and I discussed it and decided it was a bad idea."

"I'll sleep in the van with her. I don't like this movie, anyway." Janet, just graduated from fourth grade, sat up from the pallet and looked at Merry.

"Absolutely not. There are strangers out there. This hotel is right next to the freeway. Some bad man could steal you and sell you to Mexico before we even knew you were gone."

"You can't scare me," Cara said. "My mind's made up."

"I don't want a bad man to get Cara." Little Julie, always sensitive, started to cry again. If it wasn't a lost toothbrush, it was something else.

"It's okay, hush, nobody's going to get Cara. She's sleeping right here with us." Merry rubbed her youngest daughter's back.

"No, I'm not. And nobody's going to kidnap me. You can see the van from the window by the ice machine."

Jessica, Merry's oldest, the quietest and most thoughtful, asked, "Why don't you want to sleep in the room?"

"I can't share a bed with other people. I'm used to sleeping by myself."

"It won't hurt you for one night," Merry said. "And where do you plan to sleep in St. Louis?"

Cara's defensiveness was palpable. "Don't worry. I have friends."

Genevieve opened the bathroom door. "I'm exhausted," she announced. "You wouldn't think sitting in a car would wipe a body out." She yawned and stumbled across the girls' feet as Cara stood up to leave.

"She can't sleep in the van, Genevieve. Tell her."

"You can't sleep in the parking lot, sweety. Your Aunt Merry thinks it isn't safe."

"But you said I could. And you can see the van from the window by the ice machine." Cara picked up the keys from the table.

"Put those down," Merry said, sitting up.

"No," Cara said, stepping over the girls, not waiting for them to move. "My mother doesn't care, so why should you?"

"Just let her go." Genevieve pulled back the covers. "If she wants to sleep in a hot, stuffy van, that's her problem."

Merry thought her sister had completely lost her mind. "Aren't you even going to walk her out?"

"I'll be okay, Aunt Merry. See you in the morning."

As the door fell shut behind her niece, Merry got out of bed. "Where are you going?" her youngest asked, eyes still red and teary.

"I'm going to make sure she gets to the van."

"Whatever you want, little sister." Genevieve pulled up the covers and rolled over. "I need my beauty sleep."

Merry wanted to take the full ice bucket and dump it on her older sister, shock her awake in more ways than one. Instead, she kissed her girls good-night and went into the bathroom to change. She couldn't walk up and down the hall in her night gown. She changed into sweat pants and t-shirt, comfortable but presentable. "I'll be right back," she whispered to the girls. "I'm taking a key card. When the door opens, it will be me." She didn't want them jumpy or startled. She held the door so it would close gently, as quiet as a mouse click.

It was a short walk to the ice machine alcove. The long hallway swept behind toward the stairwell that was an exit. The hotel was hushed and noisy, surface silence broken by the excessive volume of a television or radio, a laugh from the lobby, a car horn somewhere, the whisper of a door falling shut, the buzz of lights, the halt and rush of water in pipes. It was ten o'clock at night and the world was still living. The ice machine clanked and ice fell inside, a liquid kind of crunch.

It was true the van was in plain sight. The automatic light was still on inside it. Cara had laid the passenger seat flat and settled herself on the middle bench so that only her blanket-covered legs were visible from the second floor. As Merry watched, the interior light dimmed and went out. She could still see what she knew were her niece's legs, though it looked like a tossed-aside blanket, a puddle of cloth that shifted with bent knees. The girl had to be sitting up. There was no way to tell if the van's doors were locked. Surely Cara wasn't that stupid. The lot was shadowy and still, impossible to see if a body moved beyond the arenas of the lampposts. When a car turned in, it traveled with no hesitation the length of the hotel, brake lights flashing as it disappeared around the corner. Another car pulled out of sight beneath the entrance's awning.

Cara was right, Genevieve was right; it was probably perfectly safe. What was she going to do, stand there all night and watch the little princess sleep? Her niece seemed to have settled in. The blanket was still visible. Merry should go back to the room, go back to bed, before the girls started to worry.

Just before she reached Room 205, a door opened half-way down the hall. A tall, skinny man stepped out, saying, "Okay, okay, I'm going to do it." When he walked past Merry, he ignored her completely. He seemed to be in a hurry.

She opened the door of their room as quietly as possible. She hoped she'd be able to sleep. The tiredness inspired by three-hundred-and-sixty-odd miles plus one adolescent pain had Merry stretched tight as a slingshot. She'd probably lie awake all night. Beauty sleep, indeed.

Room 248

Meanwhile and much earlier, L. Wentz sat in her room thinking. Oh, yes, it was his intellect, his wit, his obviously oversized brain. An encyclopedia couldn't describe his knowledge: he knew all about everything, Catholicism, Krakatoa, the Masons, *Don Quixote*, Egyptology, the gardens of Louis the Fourteenth, all the German words like *gedankenexperiment* and *Darstellung*, dozens of creation myths. Often he quoted Bertrand Russell. He said George Orwell was his secular saint. It was hard to remember all the things Andy said. Lena wished she could remember them, but if she read all the books in the world for a million years, she'd never be able to toss off analogies made up of Easter Island, Dante's *Inferno*, and the slightly hallucinogenic qualities of nutmeg. He said it was a necessity to hold many things inside one's mind at once. Well, maybe not a necessity.

What he said was, “Yeah, it’s hard to keep so many things in your head at once.” A concession to her puzzlement when once again a fascinating recombination flew right over her head. She’d once told a strange man in Palm Springs that the sexiest thing he could do while slow dancing beneath the strobe light in the bar at the Best Western would be to whisper all the names of the works of James Joyce in her ear. Even though the erect penis pressing against her abdomen was tempting, the man was no Andy. He couldn’t even name *Ulysses*.

Four years had passed, four years and two months, since Lena had last seen Andy’s face. In the meantime, they maintained a rhythm of contact via e-mail, the errant phone call when she was lucky. He was the kind of man who screened his calls, and she respected him for it. One year he called her, drunk, on Super Bowl Sunday, aroused by gladiator sports and good beer, and he got really friendly, personal, saying, “If you were here, I know what I’d do to you.” It was impossible, impossible, though they’d attempted twice before to meet, both events ending in failure. The first time a tsunami wave of guilty conscience caused her to cancel the trip, and the next time, when they planned to meet in Chicago, Andy canceled at the last minute. That had disappointed her. She vowed not to speak to him again, but four or five weeks later he sent her an e-mail, a one-liner, "Shouldn't you be shelving books?" and she laughed out loud in the middle of the Lansing Library.

The hotel wasn't funny, but it made her happy. Its sleaziness was a trumped-up affair. It was a no-tell motel, fallen from national chain status, right off the freeway in east Indianapolis. No award plaques hung behind the check-in counter.

The woman working the desk assigned her a room on the second floor and said, "Drive around back and go in Door Five." There were only a few other cars parked there. It was half past two in the afternoon. She parked before a steep bank of greenery, weedy grass, and wild shrubs.

She buzzed herself in with the key card. The hotel seemed deserted, closed doors lining empty halls with flat maroon carpeting. Her room was convenient, straight up the stairs to the right, a spacious rectangle with a window that opened onto a fantastically static-mobile view: the speeding top halves of big trucks and cars rushing south and north on I-465, the falling hillside of weeds, the shining roof of her Nissan.

She liked windows, big rooms, and a little bit of

tackiness. Someone had previously burned the lamp shade, and ripped the carpet in one place, and no doubt completely ruined a bedspread since the ones on the beds didn't match. They both had flowers in similar shades—roses, blues, purples, with green and gold scattered in—but one was abstract modern, while the other had realistic chrysanthemums. The same colors repeated in the formal stripes of the drapes. The window actually opened, sliding to the side like a patio door. This was important; she liked open windows and fresh air. The sound of the traffic was like the ocean or the wind rushing through summer trees. The ancient mini fridge seemed to work fine. A yellowing microwave sat atop it. Theoretically, a person could live here.

Lena unpacked her bag, which held very little. This was something her businessman husband had taught her. To make a hotel feel like home, spread your things around right away. Go ahead and unwrap the soap and put it in the bath-shower stall. Test the radio and find a station. Make full use of the drawers and free stationery. The room had a small round table in the corner with one nubby, maroon chair, and she made it her desk, organizing her snacks, books, and writing journal on its plastic wood-grained surface. Andy didn't get off work until

4:30—he wouldn't arrive until five—and she didn't want to just sit and wait. It was impossible, anyway. She was too uptight, an anxiety that demanded plan and action in the present. She surveyed the room before leaving it, memorizing its beautiful sordidness.

She turned left onto Shadeland Avenue and got lucky a half-a-mile later. The store was simply called "Liquor" in foot-high capital letters, the kind of place with metal grid embedded in its plate glass windows. The shelves inside were low and diagonal, no doubt for better surveillance, bright with every color of bottle and booze. In the corner, a man conversed on a phone at a Western Union machine.

Lena hadn't even known Western Union made machines. She'd never called anyone for money. The counter was a separate room in the middle of the back wall, shielded by possibly bullet-proof glass, where a woman wearing stilettos and a rump-filled skirt bought a book of stamps and a money order. To the right and left of the glass-shielded counter, the walls were defined by coolers.

Lena felt uncomfortably transparent, decidedly un-cosmopolitan; she had to make herself meet the gaze of the Western Union man when she crossed to the non-domestic section. The man looked her up and down before turning his back and getting nasty over some money transaction gone awry. He was thick-bodied, carrying weight in his gut, shaped like an arbor vitae. Andy told her he had lost forty pounds because he'd been going to gym. What kind of beer was he drinking lately? The last time, the only time, when they finally got physical, they drank cider, but not anymore; now fruit drinks gave her acid reflux. Andy probably still liked Guinness, but to her it tasted like cold, bitter coffee. Corona was too familiar, what she kept in the fridge at home. In the end, she selected Harp, two six-packs, in case they decided to stay in. She even remembered to pick up a church key, which she put down next to the beer on the counter.

The woman with the rump in the tight skirt was gone. The clerk was a pale man with a comb-over and blue eyes. He looked at her patiently, and then said, "Put it in the turnstile." The Western Union man decided at that moment to storm the counter, demanding, "She says she sent the money already." The clerk rang Lena's purchases without blinking, speaking over his shoulder to a woman who sat inside at a low desk.

She pushed a button on a microphone contraption and announced, "You just have to wait, the satellite's down." Lena paid cash for her purchase; she still had a hundred dollars. She hoped the irate Western Union man didn't notice the money, which was ridiculous. Why would anyone rob someone in front of witnesses in broad daylight?

Once again she parked behind the hotel and buzzed herself inside. The room was just as she'd left it. The door was difficult to shut this time; she had to push it hard before it latched. She still had almost two hours to kill. She should call Andy and leave a message, his voice mail was sure to be on. "I'm here," she said. "I can't wait to see you. It's Room 248." She opened a beer and stored the rest in the fridge. She wouldn't indulge recklessly; she didn't want to be drunk and bloated. One beer, and then she would take a bath, wash away the road dust.

The room had a full length mirror on the wall that had lost its lower right mooring. It drooped, creating a ripple effect that struck just above her knees. She wasn't having a good hair day. Her medium brown #5 hair had dried all frizzy, clumped; it reminded her of cotton batting. Her khaki capris were wrinkled at the crotch. Her face, from a distance, was slightly puffy—she'd gained twenty of the pounds Andy lost—but cool water and fresh make-up would make it okay. Her hair was the worst problem.

She'd brought fresh clothes, even lingerie, with the tags still on. Should she bother to wash her hair and hope it dried shinier, or dampen it and pin it back? It was the humidity that did it; it couldn't be avoided.

The latter seemed easier. She sat at the table, nursing her beer, remembering to drink it slow. Something about this meeting needed to be easy. So many tangled strings to weave, so few who would really miss her; only one, really. It was a single betrayal. She'd booked the hotel room on-line and paid cash when she arrived, so no charges would appear on any credit card or bank statements. She'd picked the Meridian Inn because it was cheap and also out of the way. She didn't want any evidence. Should she destroy the road maps with the hotel's address? It was almost a straight shot back to Lansing, highway markers clearly pointing the way.

At the check-in counter, the woman at the desk had looked at Lena's driver's license and made her sign a receipt. If her body ended up missing, her last whereabouts could be traced. Or her husband could discover them, if he ever wanted a divorce. Lena didn't want to think about it. She couldn't claim this meeting just happened. She was too old for her clothes to fall off. She stood to open the window wider. The traffic had increased in volume. Her beer was finished. She would take a bath now. She wanted to feel fresh when she saw Andy.

For a naked body, it was what it was. Not hideous for a woman her age, perhaps hideous for twenty-one, but she was no longer that. Andy once said a man could know when his wife was fooling around if she started to shave her legs, which was a complete crock—any lover she took would have to accept her, hairy legs and all. Shaving her legs was a seasonal activity. In the summer, she shaved every day, only just past her knees. She'd already done it before she left home, but she used the razor again, needing to waste time, to be extra smooth.

The last time, the only time, she'd been with Andy, she hadn't prepared at all. Had met him at a bar in grungy jeans, unshaved, in a ratty sweater she'd inherited from her teenage son. She hadn't wanted to raise any suspicions. This time, she had a whole night to spend. She could only wish for less wear-and-tear generally, but her body was what she had. It was not so terrible taken all together but if she focused too much on one part, like the sun-damaged skin above her breasts or the mosquito bite scab on her ankle, she could see its flaws. All people had bad spots: why was she obsessing? She bathed, running the water to rinse, and then dried herself off and lotioned. It still wasn't a good hair day, but a couple of bobby pins helped. The bad thing was she'd forgotten her deodorant. She put on fresh capris. She was already nervous, peeing every eight minutes. It was like waiting for a traffic light to turn, or to jump out of a plane, or the centrifugal-force ride at the carnival where the floor suddenly drops out beneath your feet. She couldn't live without deodorant. She'd have to go shopping again.

She turned left onto Shadeland Avenue, passing by the store called "Liquor." Three blocks down on the right, a mega-drugstore appeared. Did she need anything besides deodorant? Her lotion was almost gone, and she hated it, anyway, a cheap tub of milk cream that her housekeeper gave her last Christmas. She bought lotion scented like tropical waters, and also a diet Coke. There was a long line at the checkout. She spent it examining the contents of the side display, whose offerings ranged from hemorrhoid cream to lavender gum, from batteries to muscle rub. Back in her Nissan, Lena pulled out the deodorant. The scent released from her damp armpit turned sweet like baby powder.

The radio in the room was a cheap one, not digital, and somehow it had lost its station. She checked the blinking light on the phone for messages. Andy hadn't called. One more hour, and she needed music, but the radio was so hard to tune, and she stopped trying at the first plausible song, "Baby Come Back" by Player. Any kind of fool could see. She could handle a 70s station, as long as they didn't play the whiny stuff, and it was only background noise, anyway, to mix with the sounds of traffic. One more beer while she enjoyed the window with a view, and then she'd brush her teeth.

She hadn't really discussed this trip with Andy, only a quick call that lasted two minutes. What if he decided not to come? But he had said that he was free to meet her. Why did she have any doubts? It was because of the Chicago cancellation. But this time was different. Being abandoned at the last minute was always a possibility; it had happened too many times with too many people, even the ones who prided themselves on being rock solid. If he would just show up, she wouldn't wish for any more. He participated, e-mailed her, called her. He had an obligation.

She waited, sipping her beer, sitting back from the window. The single row of parking spots between the hotel and the hillside held more cars than before, mostly trucks, like the one whose door said City Wire Co, and sometimes the trucks came and left, and she started wondering what the men were doing, coming and leaving so fast, if they were picking up illegal wages or drugs, some illicit operation, and then an old red truck pulled in, three workers riding in its bed. Poor men, sitting with their arms around their knees, but maybe they were happy? The driver, a man with a thick blonde mustache, got out and entered the hotel. Her room wasn't far from the stairs. Did he have a key card? Did someone let him in? A big white truck, newer and shinier, pulled in close below her window. A single man in a black truck left. The rushing traffic was rush hour heavy. The breeze was hotter and stickier; it reminded her of childhood summers at the house in the country where they only had fans. When the knock arrived, it made her jump. She paused before the crooked mirror, and then looked through the peephole. Andy.

She always forgot how handsome he was, his nose a little crooked, the bend of his smile, brown eyes warm as mud in the sun. He looked new and improved, black leather loafers instead of canvas high-tops, a sport coat instead of a t-shirt. His crisp shirt was turquoise blue. She said, "Come in. I'm worried about all the trucks. Men keep going in and out."

Andy hadn't stopped smiling. He said, "Come here," and hugged her. Their bodies fit just right, and she couldn't help kissing his neck, it seemed so available, the skin she'd been waiting for. His warm solidness filled every inch. "I didn't know if you'd show up," she said. "And then there were all those trucks."

He went to the window and opened the curtains like he didn't care who saw him. "What trucks? I don't see any trucks."

All of them were gone, the two white ones, the black one, the red one. "I don't know. They really were there."

"I'm sure they were." He slipped off his jacket and sat down on a bed, bouncing to test its firmness. "What've you been up to? This is a surprise."

"I painted the living room last weekend. A Martha Stewart color called cornsilk."

"I've never heard of this hotel before. It's not my side of town."

"I couldn't tell from the internet. It said twelve minutes from Monument Circle."

He said, "It's a lot farther than that." He sounded disgruntled, unhappy. She didn't want to explain all the reasons she'd decided on the Meridian Inn, and so instead she offered him a beer. He made a toast to old times and old friends, and they touched their bottles and drank. When they first met, they were a whole group, and she wondered about one of the others, who at last report was teaching for Americorp somewhere in North Carolina. "Do you ever hear from Sophie?"

"Maybe once a year. She's in D.C. to get her Master's."

"In what?"

"I don't know. She was on another big kick last time I talked to her, wanting monetary reparations for slavery for African Americans. Her plan was sketchy as Vin Diesel's hair. Another one of Sophie's causes."

Lena, sitting on the opposite bed, traced an abstract flower with her finger. "I'd live in D.C. For the climate, anyway."

"I forget, what's wrong the Midwest again?"

It was a running argument, a feeling, a hunch she couldn't explain. "It's too cold. I mean weather-wise. It's too orderly or something."

"And you'd prefer a little chaos and anarchy?"

"So Manichean, Andy. I expected better."

His face smiled and he said, "Touché," raising his beer in salute.

She wanted to say something desperately important, to

ask him the mystery of love, but instead she asked, "Do you have a television yet?"

Andy shook his head. "For me, it's a tool of Satan."

Once, a long time ago, when they were taking their lunch break, they sat on a bench at the park. Nearby, the sidewalk was under repair, marked off with yellow tape. A blind man approached, and Andy noticed and asked, "Do you think somebody should help him?" She'd said no, so engaged in their conversation that she lost her capacity for mercy, whatever they were talking about, politics, books or people they hated, the places they didn't want to go or see, the things they'd never do, but Andy jumped up and approached the man, speaking to him gently, offering his arm and guiding the man around the construction zone of busted concrete. She wanted that conversation back, the intensity that was almost painful. She said, "Are you still helping blind men in construction zones?"

He wiped his forehead with the back of his hand. "Does the air conditioner work in here?"

"It does," she said, hopping up from the bed. "I like the window open, but it is a little steamy." She slid the glass shut and bent to the air conditioner, fiddling with its dial. She felt Andy moving. He was right beside her. His eyes were lowered to her mouth. She leaned in and closed her eyes without thinking. His shoulders, his back, the firmness of his arms, she'd never felt a man so hard. Inside the kiss, he was already erect. They had fit perfectly the first time, standing flat-footed in the darkness of his room. He'd wanted the lights on then, but she was too shy. She hoped this time to be braver. She pulled away and said, "Do you want the curtains open?"

He shut them. "Is that dark enough?"

"It's the best we can for the afternoon. The show must go on."

They held each other and kissed again, and then he picked her up and staggered toward the bed while she laughed and said, "Put me down, you'll hurt yourself."

She had never been good with clothes, with fumbling. She preferred to just arrive naked. He unbuttoned her capris while she unbuttoned his shirt, and she wanted not to lose the mood, but it felt self-conscious, awkward, struggling off her sleeveless sweater. His thinner body could have been marble, impressively smooth and cut, pale contours that had never seen the sun. She touched him, and his hands found her, and the slickness he discovered surprised her. He said, "What do you want?"

They were lying down and she turned her back and

cuddled into his body, moving his hands to her breasts. She swept her hair away from her neck and wrapped her arm around his waist, feeling without seeing, matching her touch to his firmness. His lips on her neck, his hand moved to her stomach, kneading the loose skin. He moved over her, and she rolled on her back, and he lay with his head on her thigh. When she came, he turned and pushed into her. At one point they rocked in unison and all parts of her disappeared, like they were floating on a planet in a unique orbit.

She and Sophie had once discussed the experience of Andy as a lover. Comparing notes, they were both surprised at his incredible stamina. Both of them had assumed that men who lived like monks would be premature ejaculators. The opposite, it seemed, was more true. She opened her eyes; he was looking at her; she tightened her thighs and touched his chest. When he came, his hips jerked three times. They lay on their backs, close, his hand covering hers. "Thank you," he said.

She kissed him, which was never disappointing. "You, too. What do we do now?"

"Do you want to go to dinner?"

She hadn't eaten all day, but she didn't feel the least

hungry. "I guess it's time. I saw a place on my way here, a restaurant with a bar and karaoke."

"I can't stay out late. I get up at five-thirty."

"I'll be right back." Lena stood and went into the bathroom, closing the door behind her. She didn't feel what she had expected. Had she thought he'd stay the night? She couldn't remember one way or the other. The plan was to get dressed and have dinner. She had to remember she was only a tourist, traveling without assumptions. She flushed and rinsed her mouth in the sink. Her clothes were scattered around the bed. She found her underwear and pulled them on. "Where do you want to eat?"

"There's a grill across the street. I saw it on my way over. It looked like the best place around." He was putting on his shorts, navy jockeys with gray elastic.

"Why aren't you wearing boxers yet?"

"Why aren't you wearing thongs?"

"Please, I might as well not wear anything."

"At least I've moved on from little boy white."

"It's about time. What are you, thirty-eight?" They dressed to conversational banter that felt too familiar. Lena did damage control on her hair. She went into the bathroom to freshen her make-up. She didn't look different, or feel different really, except maybe a little silly. What had she expected? It all seemed so mundane. Was the attraction an ontological illusion? She felt nostalgic for her husband, a very different kind of man, a longing and an absence of regret. She had to know, or she would have regretted not knowing.

"Let's go," she said once she was dressed. "Am I driving or you?"

Andy said his car was uninhabitable, and besides, it was parked way around the side. Lena drove her indigo Nissan. She missed the grill's entrance twice. The hostess said it would be fifteen minutes even though half of the tables were empty. Andy said, "Let's sit outside and smoke." She looked at him in amazement.

"I haven't started again, I just carry a pack, to remind myself I don't."

She believed him; that was Andy's kind of logic. She followed him outside and they sat on the bench. She hadn't smoked since she moved away. The cigarette tasted good.

"Let's do a gedankenexperiment," she said.

He laughed. "What's on your mind?"

"Ha, ha. You're funny. I was thinking of us in ten years."

"Us, as in the human race?"

"No. Us. You and me."

"Where are we in ten years?"

She looked at him seriously. She adored his crooked nostrils and that he was three days past needing a hair cut. "You'll have published your third novel by then and quit your job at the bank. You'll marry one of your literary groupies, a twenty-year-old with blonde hair and a boob job. They're going to come crawling out of the woodwork, you know. In ten years, you'll be swamped by tits."

"That sounds okay, but let me publish my first novel first. And don't count on the marriage thing."

"Why? Is it because you're in love with me?"

He laughed again, which was good, because she was trying to be funny. "That's probably beside the point. Where do you see yourself in ten years? Still safe behind a picket fence?"

Lena stubbed out the unexpected cigarette, reveling in her slight dizziness. The sound of traffic, the rush of commerce and cars, a shout, a distant siren. She said, "I don't know. All I'm certain of is that I'll be someplace warmer than Lansing."

"I'll never leave Indy. I have friends here, and a job I

like, and a bar around the corner from my house."

She said, "Sounds like you have it made. Maybe Indy isn't terrible."

Andy flicked his cigarette high and away down the sidewalk. "Do you think we should check on our table?"

The hostess said another fifteen minutes. When Andy pointed that the place was half-empty, she said they'd just have to wait. Lena didn't mind. She wondered at her stomach. She'd had no appetite all day. They walked back outside and Andy complained, "I feel like Kafka's prisoner, denied justice for no good reason."

"You can be Joseph K.," she said, "and I'll be Underground Man, and we can pretend we're in *Waiting for Godot*."

Andy said, "I've been reading mysteries lately." He started talking about Sir Arthur Conan Doyle, how he got sick of writing about Sherlock Holmes and killed the character off, only to be forced by his fans to bring Holmes back to life. He said, "I don't think I'm that hungry anymore. Do you want to go back and order pizza?"

"What do you really want to do?"

He looked at her. "If you didn't mind, I'd probably go home. I'm beat at the end of the day."

Who said dreams end with a whimper? A simple sentence suffices. “It’s okay. I know you’re tired. You get up at the crack of dawn.” She drove him back to the no-tell hotel and parked right next to his car. She unbuckled and got out to hug him good-bye. “Let’s not wait four years next time.”

“What’re you going to do now?”

“I don’t know. I have snacks and beer in the room. Maybe I’ll get tipsy and watch a movie.”

But that wasn’t what she did. The tacky room had lost its appeal. The radio was staticky again. She re-packed her belongings, checking all the drawers twice. She left the beer and the tub of lotion she hated. If traffic was light, she would be home by midnight to sleep in her own lonely bed.

Room 170

The first two hotels didn't have any vacancies. Ivan Peterson began to worry. His fiancée was tired of sitting in the car. His four-year-old son was getting restless. Driving the interstate with Monica and Stan strapped in, Ivan felt like they were a family and it was up to him to provide food and shelter. At the third hotel, he got out of the car and walked straight in to the counter. Monica and Stan followed behind him. His fiancée said, "Hey, I'm going to make a pit stop." He trusted that she'd take Stan. It was a good thing he'd hurried into the hotel. Two other cars had pulled in behind them.

Once they checked in and got to the room, he explained his hotel theory to Monica. Not only was an end room on the ground floor your best bet in the event of an emergency exit, but there was also the advantage of not getting trapped between two rooms of noisy strangers.

Sure, the Meridian wasn't Trump Palace, but it had forty channels of cable. The microwave was a dinosaur. In fact, he decided to unplug it. On the desk, there were coupons for local restaurants, but he didn't like half-baked spaghetti. When you ate at Wendy's, you knew what you were getting, the same French fries in Indy as in Wooster.

Monica didn't answer him. She had dumped Stan's backpack on the bed and was looking through its contents. "Did you pack the swim trunks I bought him?"

He had not only forgotten to pack them, he knew that he had forgotten, remembering the trunks a hundred miles from home. He hadn't mentioned it at the time because they were getting along, singing Itsy Bitsy Spider with Stan, and he hadn't wanted to ruin the moment. "Hey, you're making a mess over there. Playing with shoelaces again?" Ivan sat on the cheap hotel desk and crossed his arms. He had ruddy skin and large forearms with muscles that surprised and pleased him. His son was busy removing the laces from his sneakers.

"Well?" The neck of the woman he couldn't wait to marry flushed the same auburn as her hair.

"I guess I forgot. It was an accident. I'm not much of a swimmer."

"So what do you want to do instead?"

He knew he couldn't say that he wanted the same as always, dinner at a restaurant with a playground for Stan, or take fast food to a park, come back, find a movie, something with cops or detectives, watch it till Stan fell asleep, and then his turn, their turn, to play around. He had anticipated this trip for a month, their first real vacation all together. If he didn't want things to go south fast, he needed to be inventive. He said, "We could take a drive. We could drive past the Speedway, do some sight-seeing."

Monica shook her head. "I can't climb back in that car. I didn't know I hated road trips this much. Stan," she said, "do you still want to go swimming?" It was what she had whispered to the boy in the lobby to persuade him to stop jumping on the couch.

"Swimming," Stan said, waving a shoe string in the air. "But I don't have trucks."

"Trunks," Monica corrected. "That's okay, you can wear shorts."

"Okay," Ivan said. "If it's got to be swimming, then swimming it is." He didn't need to change. He was wearing a t-shirt, sandals, and shorts that exposed his pale, hairy legs.

"You're not invited, Ivan." Monica pulled out her swimsuit.

"What do you mean, not invited?"

"You don't have to do everything I do. We don't have to be together every second. Don't go to the pool if you don't like swimming. Stay here and watch sports or whatever."

"Families stick together on vacation. Didn't you read the manual?"

At that, Monica closed the bathroom door. He had only been trying to be funny. Ivan sat down at the desk and said, "Okay, Stan, give me your shoe." His son handed him a sneaker and lace.

Ivan began to rethread it as he had done a hundred times, ever since Monica had designed removing shoelaces as an activity to keep Stan occupied so he wouldn't climb up and jump on furniture. Ivan hadn't thought his son's jumping was a problem, but Monica said it broke down the springs, and more importantly, Stan might get hurt. Her younger sister's son broke his leg falling off a kitchen counter.

"Stan never climbs in the kitchen," Ivan reassured her, but she said that wasn't the point. She said, "I'm surprised you've managed to keep him alive," which

Ivan took with a grain of salt. He'd done the best he could since Stan's mother abandoned them. It wasn't easy explaining that Mommy left because she moved to Montana to live on a horse ranch with a couple she met on-line. He'd said, "Hey, Stan, it's you and me, buddy," then loneliness strung him out. He couldn't stand to be with anyone, much less his then-three-year-old son, who mostly stayed with Ivan's parents until Monica appeared on the scene.

He met her at an anniversary barbecue at Wooster Memorial Park, introduced by a friend of a friend. What struck him right away, as much as the blue shirt that showed all her curves, was the way Monica looked him right in the eyes and lifted the hair off her neck. She said, "I don't know about you, but I'm addicted to air conditioning." Her movements were as graceful as a crane carrying a two-ton I-beam. He bought her a one carat princess cut diamond as soon as he thought she'd say yes. It took six months, but the wait was worth it. Just because he didn't like water and water sports didn't mean she couldn't like them. He tried not to take it personally when he thought she was being stubborn. More than once she mentioned a hot tub, how she'd like one for cold winter nights, and even when he pointed out the expense and trouble of a hot tub, the electricity and chemical treatments, she still insisted that she wanted one.

He let the issue die. They were five years away from affording a hot tub. They weren't even married yet.

"Here, Stan. Give me the other shoe." One thing was certain as right angles, Monica was good for his son. She could get him to do about anything, eat a Brussels sprout, sleep in a bed, sit still at the barber's for a haircut. She told him, "I'm Monica. I'm not your Mama. Your Mama's in Montana. Let's draw a picture and write her a letter." She gave it to Ivan to address and mail, but he carried it around in his truck for a week until it got lost between home and one of the job sites he managed.

Ivan knew that he was a big idiot. He should have remembered to pack the swim trunks. If Monica wanted to go swimming, he'd bite the bullet and go, well, not swimming, but he'd go and sit by the pool because that's what love was about.

"I'm ready," she said, coming out of the bathroom, her arms and legs smooth and pale against the deep green, swirly-print of her swimsuit.

Ivan whistled. "Hey, sexy. Which way to the pool?"

She put her hands on her hips and spoke to Stan, ignoring Ivan's effort to seduce her.

"Come on, Mon," he said. "I'm sorry I didn't pack the trunks. How long do I get the silent treatment?" Once she hadn't talked a whole afternoon when he forgot to drop off Stan's shot records at the daycare. If he could accept her stubbornness, she ought to accept his forgetfulness.

She held Stan's hands while he slipped on his flip-flops, scrunching and wiggling his toes. "Okay," she said, "okay, okay. Tell me why you want to go to the pool."

For one, there was the safety factor; the world was full of weirdoes. "And for another thing, I want to watch you two swim while I sit back and take a tan."

Monica made a sound of disbelief and pulled a t-shirt over her bathing suit. "I don't care if you go, but we're going to stay a while. If you want to come, you can carry our towels."

He did, glad to be useful, and they walked from the end room down the long corridor of doors along the interior hall, swinging Stan between them. At the corner, they turned right to travel toward the lobby where a glass foyer behind the central staircase led to the pool deck. The desk clerk that had checked them in was talking on the phone. It was early, only three o'clock, and Ivan thought they might have the pool to themselves, but then he saw the woman lounging in the chair. Her hair was tied in a striped scarf; dark sunglasses faced the sky.

"The pool," Stan said, clapping his hands.

"The pool." Monica dropped their towels on a chair at a peachy, umbrella table. "Come on, Stan." Taking his hand, she stepped into the water.

"Cold," the boy said, stepping back out.

"It's not cold, it feels good." She knelt down and splashed a little. "See? It's fun."

The boy held onto the handrail and stepped in one foot at a time. Even on the shallowest step, the water came up to his knees.

"Come on," she said, stepping deeper until the water touched her waist. "I'll show you how to float."

"I don't want to," Stan said, stepping out.

"How do you know you don't want to? Have you ever floated?"

Ivan had seen it work before, her questioning the boy into trying things. It was really a fairly pleasant day. The sky was blue, the breeze was light, the sunlight warmed his legs. He moved the towels and propped his feet in a chair.

"I didn't float, but I ride my bike."

"Yes, you do, and you're good at it. I bet you'd be

good at floating, too."

The boy shook his head. He turned and ran a dozen steps to climb up onto a lounger.

"Don't jump. You'll fall and hurt your head." Monica touched her hair and made a face that said ouch. The boy looked and then sat down. She asked him again if he wanted to float, and once again Stan said no. "Okay," she said, like she didn't care.

Ivan had seen that strategy work, too, indifference achieving agreement. She was nothing like Susan, who cared about everything and voiced her unhappiness, or at least that's what Ivan remembered of his wife. His inability to please her was a mistake he didn't want to make twice. Monica wanted to swim, so they came to the pool; after that, it was out of his hands.

"Okay," she said, shrugging off disappointment. "I'll swim without you. Keep an eye on him, Ivan." She took a deep breath and dove under, surfaced and swam a lazy side-stroke, her graceful arms and fluid legs splashing in the water. Rolling from her side to her back and then into a breast stroke, she looked like she'd been born to swim. Ivan watched, impressed with her form, the coppery shine of her hair, the speed of her freestyle, her flutter kick, how her touch-and-roll when she reached the wall was expertly executed. Monica was full of surprises; what else didn't he know about her? The mystery of her, her sleek wet legs, the curve of her cupped white fingers, began to arouse him and he drifted into a fantasy of making love like dolphins. He forgot that he hated swimming pools. Owning her body, owning her pleasure, made him alive and invulnerable.

"Hey," the woman with the sunglasses called in an irritated voice. "Hey," she called and pointed. Ivan looked and saw his son struggling underwater. He leaped up and splashed down the steps, caught Stan's arm, jerked him into the air, slippery and cold, coughing and sneezing.

Monica was right there, asking, "What happened? What happened?"

"What happened," Ivan said, climbing up the steps, his shorts and sandals dripping, "I don't know. Stan fell in."

The boy was curled against his father's chest like a rescued kitten, his ear against Ivan's heart. Silvery snot dripped from his nose. His breathing had the rhythm of hiccups.

"Fell in?" she said. "What do you mean, fell in? Where was he standing when it happened?"

She was dripping too, her crossed arms plumping up

her breasts, the exposed skin dimpled with goose bumps. Ivan held the boy securely with one hand and with the other picked up a towel, flapped it open, and wrapped it around his son's body, wiping the boy's nose. "By the stairs, I think, no, on the stairs."

"By the stairs or on the stairs? Weren't you watching him, Ivan?"

"I was watching. He was on the stairs, okay? He was standing right there, and then he just leaned over and fell in." Ivan didn't mean to feel angry, but all he could think was: what if he'd stayed in the room? There she'd be, swimming away, and Stan would have drowned. She ought to be thanking him, calling him a hero; he'd dived in and saved his son's life.

"Are you okay, buddy?" Monica asked, touching Stan on the chin.

The boy nodded yes and started to cry, his blue eyes turning liquid. He shivered and cuddled closer to Ivan. "We're going back to the room," Ivan said. "Stay and swim, since that's what you wanted."

He didn't care if it hurt her feelings. She said, "Ivan, you're being ridiculous." She pulled on her t-shirt and collected her towel.

The woman in the sunglasses watched them go. She'd

sunned on her back long enough. Gracefully, smoothing her towel, she rolled over on her stomach.

Much later, a few minutes after nine that night, Stan finally fell asleep. When they had first returned to the room, Monica offered to stay with the boy and bathe him, a nice warm bubble bath, while Ivan went to pick up dinner, but he said no, he would stay with Stan while she went out to a drive-through for French fries and burgers. "You've done enough already," he said. "I'll give him his bath tonight."

He regretted the words once she was gone. He tried to make it up to his son. He pretended the soap was a flying fish, dipping and tickling Stan's body. He settled them together on the bed closest to the television and let Stan have the remote, showing him which button to push to make the frequency turn. After Stan had flipped through six or seven times, with stops on commercials and random channels—QVC, CNN, Discovery, the soap opera network—Ivan gave him a tennis shoe and took the remote away. Selecting the channel that was showing back-to-back episodes of *Law and Order*, Ivan pulled out a canvas bag packed with Stan's toys and settled back to wait.

When he heard Monica fumbling at the door, he got up and let her in. "Hi," he said. "Welcome back. What did you decide to bring us?"

"The usual," she said, carrying in two sacks and setting her purse on the dresser. "Hey, Stan, how you feeling?"

"The turtle holds hands with Spiderman." Ivan's son held up two figures, their arms pressed together.

"Where are they going?"

"To the baseball," he answered, surprising Ivan, who hadn't thought the kid was paying attention. Tomorrow they'd be in St. Louis to watch the Reds play the Cardinals. Ivan was given the gift of free tickets from one of the electrical supply houses he did business with, not only free tickets but a night in the company condo to go with them. Getting things free was one pleasure of the trip; he hoped Monica appreciated his connections.

She didn't act like she was angry. He couldn't tell what she was feeling. She unpacked fast food at the table. "That's right, we're going to see a baseball game. Come on, Stan, say, 'Go Reds'."

She scooped the boy up and sat him in a chair to eat his burger, fruit, and milk. She handed the other sack to Ivan. "Here, I asked for double cheese."

“Thanks,” Ivan said, his stomach grumbling. With all the commotion of swimming and saving Stan’s life, he hadn’t realized he was starving.

Now sleeping, Stan looked larger than life, a resting four-year-old giant, long and solid, full of air. On a commercial break, Ivan lowered the volume and sat up, swinging his feet to the floor. “Hey,” he said. “Thank you.”

“For what?” Monica looked up from her magazine. After they’d eaten, she’d taken a shower and put on her pajamas, a white cotton set with a v-neck t-shirt and shorts. Her face, scrubbed clean and sun touched, was irrevocably serious.

“Thanks for a great night,” he said. “Everything turned out fine. Look at our boy. He’s down for the count.” Assorted action figures, cars, crayons, the tiny rubber lizards they’d bought at the zoo: Ivan picked up the toys scattered on and under the covers. He tossed the remote to Monica. “Here, watch what you want. My show’s over now.”

Monica sat the controller on the nightstand. “I don’t care about TV. I’m reading. And then I’m going to sleep.” She was sitting in the center of the opposite bed, her magazine propped on her knees.

Ivan dropped the last of the toys into the canvas bag and stored it next to his suitcase. "It's early. We don't have to go to sleep yet." He sat down on the bed next to her, reaching for her hand, but she squeezed, let go, and said, "I'm not in the mood, Ivan."

She sat there so irresistible, her calves smooth and curved as moons, the spot on her neck like a star where he kissed it. "Lady, are you still mad at me?"

"I don't want to talk about it, I'm tired. I might say something I'd regret."

She wouldn't even look at him. He always said—she knew how he felt—that people shouldn't go to bed mad. "I don't understand, Mon. I thought when you brought dinner back, we were going to have a good night."

"It was fine," she said quickly. "I was happy to see Stan eat all his mandarin oranges."

She fell silent and turned a page in her magazine. Ivan looked back at the TV. It was a *Law and Order* episode he had seen before, a woman who disappears and then they find her body. The character was having an affair. Her lover was the murderer. They caught him because of a half of a phone number scrawled on a piece of paper. Ivan had had one wife disappear. Her absence left him hollow. What was he supposed to do, act like he didn't care when Monica wouldn't speak to him? "Hey," he said, "I don't want to be the kind of man who can't keep a woman like you."

She looked at him deliberately and blinked. "That's nice, Ivan. Can we talk about it in the morning?"

"What's wrong with tonight? I love you, Mon."

"Tonight I'm tired. Let's just sleep, okay?"

"When I say I love you, you're supposed to say it back."

"If you don't know that I love you by now, saying it's not going to make you believe it."

He knew what it was about. "It's about the pool, isn't it? It's because of the swim trunks. You know that I forget things."

"It's not just the trunks. Forget them all you want."

What was it then, he had to know. In her steady pose, she was all that he wanted. "Monica, I want to make love to you."

She closed her magazine and put it down. She crossed her arms and said, "That was never going to happen. Stan's in the same room."

"He's sound asleep. He won't wake up."

"I wouldn't do it, anyway, Ivan, not if we were on another planet."

"Why? What's going on with you?"

"Because I still don't understand why it was my fault when Stan fell in the pool."

He wanted to answer that it was partly her fault. She was the one who wanted to go swimming. But it was also partly an accident. Ivan seemed to attract them. He said, "It's nobody's fault. Everything's fine. Look at him, he's already forgotten about it."

"If it's nobody's fault, why were you so hateful? I don't like to be talked to that way."

"I was just upset. Look, he almost drowned. I must have been in shock."

She said, "I know, don't you think I know? Do I get to feel shocked, too? I still don't understand how it happened."

She didn't know because she was swimming and not paying attention. Ivan had a theory. "He was trying to copy you. He saw you swimming and he wanted to swim like you."

"I didn't even know he was near the pool."

"He was watching, and then he got on the steps, and then he just fell in."

"I don't understand how that's my fault. Because I wanted to swim to begin with?"

She was over-analyzing, caring too much; he hadn't meant anything by it. "You're right, it wasn't your fault. If it was anyone's fault, it was mine." In his heart, he'd say anything just to get close to her. He wanted to put the brakes on the argument.

"I can't get over it that fast. I feel insulted, Ivan. To tell you the truth, I wish I hadn't left Wooster."

"I guess we won't be sleeping together then. Now you're going to punish me."

Monica sighed, sat up, agitated, pulled loose her knotted-up hair, gathered it again and refastened it with a twist.

How could she not feel how she aroused him, the blush beneath her upraised arm, the way she rolled her eyes, her discontent that would surely dissolve if only he could touch her. "All I wanted was to hold you until you fell asleep."

"Why?" she asked. "Why?"

"Because I love you," Ivan said, "and we're going to be married in a month, and I want to get used to sleeping in the same bed." The hotel would be their first time. Back in Wooster, they both slept at home because it seemed the right thing to do and to avoid giving people a reason to talk.

She sighed and pushed Ivan to stand up. "Okay, then, but go around. This is my side."

Once they were in the darkness, he couldn't help himself. He tried to lie still and breathe with her breathing, but his hands would not stay still. She squirmed and pushed against him, which only made it worse, until she sat up and turned on the light. "Ivan, no means no."

"I know, Mon, but you feel so good. Come on, we'll be quiet."

"Ivan, I said stop it. Either get in the other bed, or I will."

She wouldn't let him wash her laundry. She always locked the bathroom door. She didn't like holding hands or kissing in public. She didn't always answer her cell; she said she didn't hear it ringing. "Monica, we can't go on like this."

She groaned and shrugged her shoulders. "Just stop. If we were back in Wooster, it'd be time to hang up the phone."

Soon enough they'd be living in the same house, and what did she plan to do then? "Something's happening. I think we might have a problem."

"Yes," she said, standing up between the beds. "The

problem is, Ivan, you have to learn to live with problems. Everything can't be solved with a snap of your fingers."

"Love. Love can solve all problems."

"Right, Ivan, you're absolutely right."

He'd lost the gist of the argument and now she was being sarcastic. "I don't understand what your problem is."

"You should have stayed in the room. Then I would have been watching Stan. I can't help it, he almost drowned." Monica looked down at him. "I'm going to the bathroom. I need to brush my teeth."

In her back, he saw the emblem of abandonment. "That's what you always do. You run, Monica. Hang up the phone, brush your teeth. The problem is, you don't care enough to get to the bottom of anything. You're shallow as a puddle."

Monica stopped and turned around. He tried to backtrack, but she interrupted. "No," she said, "don't apologize. This time you hit it on the nose." She shook her head with realization. "I'm shallow, and you're deep, and we're never going to get along. This isn't the first time. Haven't you noticed?"

"What?" he said, standing up, but she held him at bay with raised hands. "You're just upset, it's a stupid fight."

"No. I mean it. I don't think I can marry you. We're just too different, Ivan."

They weren't different. They were just the same. They agreed on all kinds of plans, having another kid, hopefully a girl who Monica wanted to name Lily. Working hard toward retirement, which secretly he wanted to be somewhere warm, Arizona or Florida, though she always said she'd never leave Wooster. But that was years ahead of them; they'd worry about that when they got to it. "Monica, you don't mean it. What about the future?"

Instead, she took off the one carat ring, which hadn't even been sized, and set it on the dresser. He wanted her to wear it on the trip so he could admire it on her finger. To make it fit, he wrapped the band with tape, which looked grubby now, dirty and worn.

"Please," he said. "I was one hundred percent wrong."

"No," she said. "There are things I can never say to you. There are things you'll never understand." She looked around as if something were lost that she couldn't lay her eyes on. "I don't think I can stay here tonight."

"That's crazy, where are you going?" Would it be his fault if she walked away? Every woman he ever loved left him.

"No," she said, pulling out shorts and t-shirt, slipping them over her pajamas.

"What if Stan wakes up and asks where you are?" Monica was heartless, thoughtless, she was just like his ex-wife, putting on her clothes and shoes, throwing shampoo in her toiletry bag, and zipping up her suitcase.

She hesitated, weakening, but she sniffed away the tears. "Tell him I'll be back for breakfast. Tell him we'll have pancakes."

When she left, Ivan collapsed on the sheets. The plain white pillow case smelled like nothing. Too late, he jumped up and flung open the door. The corridor was empty.

⁛ Front Lobby ⁛

I.

When the sun went down, the Meridian Inn's sign lit up, white with black lettering. The name was written in brush script and accented with the icon of a carriage lamp, a nostalgic image that clashed with the Mediterranean stucco of the hotel's exterior, not to mention the Roman Tuscan columns of the entry bay. Inside the lobby, beneath the illumination of recessed can lights and the three ancient chandeliers, Duncan confirmed a guaranteed late arrival. "Hey," the guest, Phillip E. Stephenson, said, "how late is the pool open? The kids think they want to go swimming."

The kids were outside the lobby doors running circles around an aging minivan, its side dimpled like it had been used for a backstop, the brats hyped up, no doubt, on caffeine, French fries, and sugar, the holy trinity of an

American diet. Duncan wanted to respect kids in general, but he'd experienced one too many in his life: fat ones, skinny ones, sulky ones, smelly ones, thumb-sucking, skirt-hugging, snotty-nosed, screaming, puking, cute-as-hell kids. Poor Stephenson, soft-bellied in his drooping denim shorts, his pitted face creased with wrinkles. Pathetic, really, old before his time, his greatest pleasures no doubt reduced to internet porn or losing sports teams. According to his cap, he was a Cubs fan. "The pool closes at eleven. Sign here, Mr. Stephenson."

Stephenson slid his license into his wallet and picked up his receipt. "Hey, can you leave the pool open all night? Maybe I could get some shut eye."

Duncan forced a laugh of camaraderie and waved a quick back-and-forth with his hand, ending in a shooting motion. Poor slob; if he'd seen it once, he'd seen it a million times, some average guy who would be perfectly happy if he weren't chained by kids and marriage to drudgery, mired in the misery of family life, the soul-damaging cycle of dysfunction repeating. It could happen to anyone, even Duncan's mother, chained to the ass of his father, a fierce descendant of Highland Scots on the one side and draft-dodging Southern Germans on the other. His ancestors always fought on the side of Right and Truth. Except his father, who was something of a fascist, but well, there you go. Life is not a bowl of sweetened cream, not even for the terribly gifted and kind. Duncan did his best to move onward and upward.

"Darn kids," he added for Stephenson's parting benefit.

A stout man in brown shorts and black socks crossed the lobby to the vending machines. Beyond the machines, Duncan could see the vacant swimming pool area glowing with unearthly blue light. Duncan didn't go in for swimming, but he could admire the aesthetics of chemically-adulterated water, its swirls shimmering fluorescent against shining blue tiles.

From the back wing, a woman emerged pulling a suitcase. She was one of those fair women, strawberry blondes, a red head dressed in pink, a young Ann-Margret, or maybe Ann-Margret's country cousin. When she veered toward the desk, Duncan straightened his tie. She stopped and let go of the suitcase. "Hello," she quavered. "Can I get another room?"

Up close her nose was as pink as her t-shirt, blotchy instead of creamy. She sniffed once, her blue eyes shot with tears.

"Another room. Does that mean you already have a

room?" Her red hair was thick as ribbon, pulled up in a ponytail.

She sniffed hard twice, brushing her eyes with neatly, unpolished fingertips. "It's not the room; it's who's in the room."

It wasn't the first time an unhappy woman stood on the other side of the desk. Duncan could only be relieved that she didn't break down completely, snotting and sobbing all over the lobby. When that happened, all he could ever do was offer a tissue or maybe a pat on the shoulder. He understood that crying women needed comfort, but over-familiarity made him uncomfortable. "I hope everything's okay. It's not an emergency, is it?"

"It feels like an emergency." She held up her bare left hand. "I broke up with my fiancé. He wouldn't let me get any sleep."

Duncan mentally cuffed himself on the forehead: what kind of bonehead was he? "Let me see what rooms I have available." He perused the possibilities. A single wanting a single. He felt like a matchmaker here. The sad, sexy woman aroused his sympathy. The break-up wouldn't have been her fault. Her fiancé was probably a dunderhead Republican, one of those jerks who yelled racial epithets at basketball games and/or sucked Bill

O'Reilly's rhetorical dick.

But the room situation didn't look good. In the upper back, he had a few doubles, all of them designated smoking. The front wing was pretty well taken or reserved. Room 233 was marked for repairs, another one off the roster. There was the lower back wing, but the woman deserved something better.

The state of the back rooms in general depressed Duncan: dingy and soul-deadening as his garage apartment; wired together like his ancient Toyota truck; as sad as the fact that a loaf of bread always molded before he could eat the whole thing unless he stored it in the refrigerator which turned the bread stale; all he asked for were smaller loaves; the student loans he still owed six years out of college; the degree he had never quite achieved: what did geometry have to do with history, anyway?

"I'm looking," he said, "but it's not good. What if I give you an executive suite at a special discount rate?" It was the least he could do for a runaway bride.

"How much is that?"

She sounded interested without being convinced that a suite was entirely affordable. He played around with discounts, just to make it official, corporate, senior, disabled, military, then offered her the lowest regular rate. "Sixty-four dollars plus tax. It's one of the best rooms we have."

"What about one that's not the best? Do you have anything cheaper?"

From the back wing, Elaine emerged. She had been on a housekeeping mission. Simultaneously, a rangy man started down the stairs. The Stephenson kids skipped from the lower front hall racing for the pool in their swimsuits, a tired-looking woman following behind, shouting, "Walk, don't run. I said, walk. Turn your listening ears on."

Duncan contemplated the availabilities. It was a disappointment that the defecting bride hadn't snapped up his executive offer. A woman who could participate in the high tragedy of a busted engagement should have the emotional wherewithal to perform irrational financial gestures, heightening the drama, selling the pig with the barn, in effect, throwing out the baby in the rain. Sixty-four bucks plus taxes, and she could celebrate the loss of her engagement in style.

"We have other rooms, but they're smoking. Are you interested in one of those?"

She bit her bottom lip and shook her head. "I'd rather

have non-smoking. I don't like the smell in my hair."

Elaine joined Duncan behind the desk. "Hey," she said. "I'm off at eleven? Everyone has a pillow."

The rangy man had reached the desk. Duncan recognized him from earlier. "Can you help Mr. Wildrick first? I'm busy over here."

The indirection didn't make Elaine happy. He could tell by her silent snarl. Maybe she was scheduled to leave at eleven but she knew it didn't work that way, and to top it off, she'd been late again, the log-in said almost an hour, not to mention that her replacement, Ryan, wasn't coming in. He'd called and said he broke his arm, a verifiable excuse, unlike the redundant headache or stomach virus that regularly struck Elaine. Wildrick probably needed something minor, a wake-up call or more towels.

Instead, what he said caused Duncan to look up from his contemplation of rooms and ex-brides. Duncan had had Wildrick, a near giant, pegged as the upright type, button-down shirt and wire-rimmed glasses, conventional little-boy haircut, probably a computer guy, or maybe a car rental agent. The woman, Wildrick's wife, if he remembered correctly, was a smaller, female version of Wildrick, as neutral as the color beige, the pair together as articulated as the texture of used sandpaper.

"We're, I guess we're, having a little problem. We need another room."

"Good luck," said the red-headed woman. "All they have is smoking."

"At this point, I'll take whatever they've got."

Elaine frowned. "What room are you in now? Maybe we can fix the problem."

"I'd rather not. It's nothing, really. Don't worry, I'm willing to pay."

"We do have rooms besides smoking," Duncan added. "There are the executive suites."

The phone rang, an outside line. Elaine picked it up in a flash.

"How much is an executive suite?" Wildrick thumbed through his wallet.

The red-headed woman gripped the handle of her suitcase. "What's wrong with the room you have now? I just need a place to sleep."

Wildrick looked down at her, his blue eyes baffled behind super-thin lenses.

Duncan said, "If you want an executive suite, we have one available, but I'll still have to process the switch. What's going on? Air conditioning problems? Noise?"

"No, nothing like that. It's my wife. Let's just say it's nothing."

Elaine put the call on hold; she seemed in a better mood. "If we know the problem, we can file a maintenance report." She beamed her brightest, tadpole-eyed smile.

Wildrick barked a nervous laugh, high-pitched for a man of his stature. "I don't know if that would help. The thing is, well, the thing is. I'll take an executive suite."

"He told me sixty-four dollars plus tax," the red-headed woman put in.

"Sixty-four dollars? What kind of rate is that?" Elaine put her hands on her hips.

Duncan was liking the ex-bride less and less as seconds and minutes ticked by. Maybe her dunderhead Republican fiancé was really a nice guy who had made a simple request, something not too kinky, like wanting to suck her toes or asking her to lick his nipples, and she went all Puritan and threw the engagement ring at him. She had a saintly air. She wouldn't look half-bad in a habit. "We can get started on the switch as soon as you give me a reason."

"Okay," Wildrick said. "If you have to know. The room, well, my wife thinks it's haunted."

Why was it the most normal-looking people who turned out to be the weirdest? Who in their righteously scientific mind still believed in spirits? "Haunted, huh?"

"Things keep moving around. Like the chairs. They're here," Wildrick held out his arms from the waist, extended with palms vertical, impersonating furniture. "And the next thing you know, they're here." He swung his arms a scant inch at an angle.

"Can you see them move?" Elaine looked interested and, not for the first time, Duncan disdained her friendliness. Why encourage the guests, why breach the good wall between the personal and the professional?

"Not really. It doesn't happen when we watch."

The man spoke with all seriousness. It didn't hurt that Wildrick was tall. Tall men historically achieved instant credibility—Lincoln, de Gaulle, John Wayne. Duncan thought of the legendary general Hannibal, tall, mean, and elephant-riding, slaughtering thousands, but he never took Rome. He asked, "How do you know it happens if you can't see it?"

Wildrick laid down his credit card. "You can tell by the dents in the carpet."

The man was willing to pay. He had a legal right to rent as many rooms as he could afford. Duncan began the transaction.

The ex-bride listened with interest, nodding. "I still wonder, could I have the room? Ghosts aren't one of my problems. I figure, what I don't believe in can't hurt me."

Score a point for the bride who wasn't getting married. Duncan had had stranger nights. There was the time when a guest shot off three toes, a lethal mixture of drunkenness and suicidal tendencies that added up to a miracle. In his drunken misery, the genius had pointed the rifle at his foot instead of at his brains. "If Mr. Wildrick says you can have his room, we can make the adjustment. I'll need to see your driver's license."

Her name was Monica LeMaire, an Irish-French combination, easy on the eyes but no Marian Carravejo; she didn't have the same backbone or serene sensibility.

"Here you go," Elaine said, handing a key card to Wildrick. "You might want to move your vehicle. You need to enter through Door Three. The suites have a private entrance."

Wildrick left, wishing Monica good luck. "I hope you get some sleep."

"I always sleep like a baby," she answered.

Duncan didn't doubt it. The ex-bride now struck him as simple and practical, no doubt industrious and animated on occasion, but, at the end of the day, the kind of woman who picked wash-and-wear over cashmere, hot chocolate over aged Scotch whiskey, the movie version of *Jane Eyre* over the novel. “Here you go,” he said. “You’re all set. You might want to give Mr. Wildrick and his party a few minutes to clear out.”

Monica walked across the lobby and settled on a sofa.

“So, Duncan,” Elaine said. “Let’s talk about when I’m getting off work.”

The hold light still flashed red. “Is that a guest?”

“It’s personal. Don’t worry about it.”

Elaine was competent at many things, but she had no vision of the bigger picture. “I hate to tell you, but Ryan broke his arm. I’ll need you until at least midnight.”

She protested, “I bet he broke it on purpose. I can’t stay late tonight.” But Duncan held his ground.

“I need you to stay until the pool’s closed and the night audit’s further along.”

Elaine glared at him and gave up. “Aye, aye, Captain Bligh. Can I at least take my personal call in the office?”

He didn’t want to be a complete hardass. He didn’t want to become his father. You fight against the Man until one day you become the Man. Monica LeMaire headed for the elevator. “Go ahead, but hurry it up. The sooner we get the reports started, the sooner you can leave." Headlights flashed in the parking lot.

Across the lobby, the Stephenson kids splashed up a wild old time in the pool. If he had to choose between ghosts and kids, he'd take the ghosts every time. They didn't spill Kool-aid, wet their pants, or scream when they had to go to bed.

Marian had hinted she wasn't crazy about children. Once she said, "The world doesn't need more kids whose parents don't want to raise them."

He didn't think the world needed that, either. It was another idea on which the two of them agreed. He wondered what Marian would think of the ghost. They'd never discussed the supernatural. As soon as the ex-bride had time to settle in 212, he planned to call and check on the room. In the meantime, he watched the Stephenson kids splashing. They were a remedy to the green grass theory; things weren't always rosier on the other side.

II.

When Elaine flipped on the lights in the office, fluorescence lit up the dirty windows. She could see herself, a reflection of the situation, a short woman with tired, spiky hair. She flashed a big smile, happy lips and bared teeth. Then she dropped the blinds, shutting off the reflection and twisting the louvers for privacy. At the nearest desk, she plopped into a rolling chair. If she had three wishes, the first would be that she was on a plane to Paris with Portia de Rossi, whom Karen didn't even resemble. Instead, she picked up the phone to talk to her girlfriend. "Hey," she said, "I'm here now. Tell me, what did you find?" At least Karen was still at home. Spinning around in the gray box of the office, Elaine kicked off her shoes and stretched her tired feet.

"I've been waiting forever. You know I don't like to wait."

"It's crazy here. I can't tell you. I have maybe five minutes."

"Guess what I found in the boxes."

Elaine didn't want to guess, a long, boring game, but in the end, a few tries was less effort. The red dress? That wasn't it, and neither was an invasion of ants, or the past due electric bill, a guess that caused Karen to say, "You're no good at guessing. I don't think you're really trying."

Elaine said, "No, I'm trying, but you're right, I'm no good. Why don't you just tell me?"

"It starts with a J."

"Gym socks?"

"That starts with G. Think of J, like jail bird."

"Don't tell me, you found something illegal." If it was anything that would hurt her mother, Elaine would dispose of it. Her mother deserved a peaceful retirement. She'd been through a lifetime of troubles.

"No, it's jewelry. Amazing jewelry, Laney. Clip-on earrings with huge, emerald rhinestones and a matching necklace and bracelet. And these dangly earrings that look like they're made of aluminum strings."

Karen had opened four of the five boxes that were Elaine's dead great-aunt's remains. A million years ago, Great-aunt Miriam had been Miss Indianapolis in the State Fair Queen's competition, her photograph taken in a large crown and red satin dress, the one Karen hoped to find because Great-aunt Miriam was similar in figure, slender, tall, flat-footed.

"I bet this ring is worth something. It's amethysts and gold. And there's a costume pearl necklace, in its original case. Listen." A popping-snapping sound clapped from the phone. "That's how tight the springs are."

They really shouldn't have opened the boxes. What would her mother say? Elaine hated Florida when she flew down to visit; the retirement community felt like temporary housing on land reclaimed from swamp and quicksand. The genetically-engineered grass freaked Elaine out with its sharp-edged, plastic nature. “Don’t start selling my great-aunt’s jewelry. Those boxes belong to my mom.”

“I’m not going to sell anything. I just want to wear them. You’re the one who won’t come home.”

It wasn’t worth the effort to explain again the difference between employment and homelessness. “I’ll be there in an hour, promise.”

“Okay, but that’s it. There’s one more box to open, anyway.”

“So, you’re staying home?”

“In an hour, I’ll make up my mind.”

“Just call if you decide to go out, can you at least do that?”

“Yeah, sure. I love you, Laney.”

Elaine hung up and found her shoes, forced her small feet back into them. If she had any choice, she’d walk out right now, on the Meridian, on Duncan, on Marian, on Housekeeping, on every fricking guest who’d ever complained about ghosts, hot water, flat pillows, weak internet connections, cold heating or hot air conditioning, damp towels, spiders, roaches, dusty baseboards, or mildewed bath tiles. She'd quit and go home before her girlfriend went out and sold her mother's inheritance, getting drunk in the process and hooking up with some sleazy chick at the Bulldog. If Elaine had any free will, she would walk out on everything. But she couldn't let go, of her lover or the job. She was in love and needed the money.

Room 233

East of the freeway, a neighborhood sprawls in a crossword puzzle of streets. The houses crowd together with driveways like alleys edged by overgrown trees and shrubs. A slight wind is blowing. Sometimes there's a fence. He remembers the flowers growing by a fence that he used to pick and pull out the stem to get a drop of honey. From the side yards, the odor of garbage drifts, and from the traffic, exhaust mixed with noise. It is one of those nights when the sky over the neighborhood hangs low, pressing the darkness deeper into the spaces between the houses. Over time, the houses have added rooms and enclosures, gables, garages and additions, though the house that Gus inhabits with what is known as his family hasn't had any improvements.

Kercheval Drive is deserted when he steps from the corner to cross the vacant lot near Fifty-Second Street.

The traffic's volume increases as he follows a rough path worn through the vacant field. What he can remember is stored in locked closets in boxes on shelves of descending stairs. His hand in his pocket holds the disconnected cell phone that he continues to keep charged and with him. He holds a thin belief that someday it will ring when he least expects it. When the phone opens, the screen flashes: *I hate wat it du.*

He steps onto the sidewalk at the curve leading to the underpass. From the alley next to the old Mobile station, a voice makes him stop.

"What up, Gus?"

"Hey."

"Where you going?"

"Hell if I know." He walks in the darkness, not toward a purpose but in the opposite direction. The appearance of Jesse with Allisandra seems as natural as the sequence of events that has led him onto the streets to begin with. "What up with you?"

"Got any weed?"

"Naw, I'm dry, man."

"Do you wanna smoke?"

A car exits the freeway and curves down the ramp, its headlights flashing in their direction. "Let's get the fuck off the corner, anyway."

The three join company, walking west toward the underpass. The purse of Allisandra, who is delicate and dark-haired, bumps against her right hip. "Hey, Gus," she shouts against the roaring traffic. I-465 is above them.

"Hey." Since Gus met her, sitting in math class in high school, Allisandra has been the same, quick to speak out, making people laugh, always trying to be funny. She isn't beautiful; her face is too long and her eyes droop at the corners. Though once they ran in the same circles, Gus doesn't meet up with her often. Jesse is one step further removed, still in school and living with his mother and grandmother in an apartment near Fall Creek.

"So," Jesse says, looking over his shoulder, "you still work at the Meridian?"

"Yeah. I don't know how long."

"How about you get us a room?"

He hasn't been thinking of his job. The tunnel of the underpass is a thunderous cave, trembling in both directions. Jesse says something, but it's lost in the heaving roar. On the other side, the street is clear, so they cross before they get to the corner.

Jesse stops and taps out a cigarette, offering it to Gus. "Come on, man, a hotel room. Don't you got a pass key or something?"

"We have vodka." Allisandra lifts her purse. "In the hotel, they have cups and ice."

Cars travel up and down Shadeland, bunching together at red lights. The stores in the strip mall across the street are closed, the dry cleaner's window lit by a blue neon hanger that says, "One Hour Martinizing." Gus lights up. "Give me a drink."

"Right here? Somebody will see."

"No problem. I'll turn around." He holds up his hands and turns a half-circle so his back faces the street.

Jesse says, "If you want a room, give him the bottle."

It's a glass pint, its seal cracked, and he turns it up easy and swallows, bottoms up like warm kerosene, a trail burning his throat to his stomach.

"Hey, man, save some for us."

He stops and gives up the bottle to Jesse, wiping his mouth with the back of his hand. In the reflective air, Allisandra's skin looks blue. "We can get a room, but not all night."

"My mother would kill me. I have to be home by two." Allisandra slips the bottle back in her purse. "I can't believe we're doing this." Across four lanes, a car turns south, tires squealing and music booming from its system.

From the north, they travel toward the Meridian. Gus lets them into the remote entrance of the front wing using the key card he forgot to turn in. Allisandra's round hips flex in low-slung jeans, exposing a candy-pink thong that Gus follows all the way up the stairs. The hallway is deserted. They could have had a room in the back, but 233 is better because he knows it's off the roster. "This one," he says, opening the door and flipping on the lights.

"Nice." Allisandra sits on the bed and bounces. "What's wrong with that mattress?"

"Somebody took a piss." He crosses the room and opens the window, pulling the drapes almost closed. Jesse sinks down close to Allisandra, moving in for a kiss, but she laughs and bounces and pushes him away.

"Not yet. First, I want to drink and smoke. Why don't you get us some ice?" She stands up and opens her purse on the dresser.

"I'll get it." Gus takes the bucket. "You can look for something on TV. It has Discovery Channel."

"Does it have porn? I want to see some skin." Jesse hunches forward, holding the remote and flipping through the channels.

Allisandra looks at him with one eye wide. "Don't be

a jerk. I might have to dump you and go out with Gus."

"Yeah, right. You know you like it."

Gus leaves, closing the door. The hallway is a striped golden tunnel with a floor of reddish moss. Although it has no windows, it is different than during the day. Behind each door is not a used, empty room waiting to be stripped and cleaned, but people sleeping or doing the kind of things people do behind walls. The ice machine's engine buzzes in the alcove. He sets the bucket lid on the windowsill.

A door down the hallway opens and shuts. A man's voice says, "This way." Gus freezes, waiting, but the couple turns in the opposite direction to head toward the distant stairwell. The whispered tone of the woman's voice is incredulous. She can't believe something that has just happened. She asks a question that trails away and then they make their exit.

Gus looks toward the landing and down the hall. Holding the full ice bucket close to his chest, he walks back to the room. Allisandra has unwrapped the cheap glass tumblers and arranged them on the dresser. He locks the door and puts down the ice. "Okay, let's get this party started."

They smoke a blunt and drink vodka, the couple sitting

on the one good bed, Gus in a chair that he moves so it's close and facing the TV. Allisandra sits with her arm twined through Jesse's, massaging his leg. "I've only been in one other hotel," she tells them. "When I was little, we went to Cincinnati because my grandmother died, and my father got drunk and couldn't drive home. My aunt wouldn't let us stay at her house, so we had to get a hotel. It was bad because my mother got mad, and my father wouldn't stop crying. She kept saying, 'What a waste,' meaning the money it cost, because he never went to see his mother when she was alive."

Jesse passes the blunt to Gus. "He probably had his reasons. Waste is in the mind of the beholder. Check this out." He takes her hand curled inside of his and presses it to his heart. "Allisandra, will you waste a little time with me?"

Her laughter is like the surprise when a twenty-dollar bill falls from the piñata. "You're funny. Stop it." But she doesn't push Jesse away, instead kisses his cheek. It's the go-ahead he's been waiting for.

Gus looks away from the couple. Roiling, the smoke rises and curls toward the speckled white ceiling. The vodka is diluted with ice, weaker and easier for being cold. On TV, a man on a riverbank says, "The deeper an

American toad's call, the better chance it has of attracting a mate." The sound of croaking accompanies a picture of bug-eyed toads with swollen throats like blue speckled balloons.

"Hey."

"What?" Gus hits the blunt and passes it.

Jesse gestures toward the door. "Why don't you take a walk? Give us a little privacy."

Allisandra smiles, sips her drink, and sits the cup on the nightstand.

"Where am I supposed to go?"

"I don't know. Where were you going to start with?"

"Hell if I know." Gus finishes the last of his drink in one short swallow.

On TV, the man stands in a dark wood with a little spotlight on his face while behind him toads croak loudly. He says, "Individual signals must therefore be distinct and stand out clearly from the background noise."

"There are too many lights." Allisandra turns off the one between the beds and walks to the switch by the door. When she sits back down, she sits close to Jesse. Without saying anything, she turns his face with her hands and raises her lips. Her eyes are closed, her dark hair falling forward against the fullest part of her t-shirt.

The man on the TV says, "Small toads can change the pitch of their call by sitting in cooler parts of the pond." When Gus turns his head, he sees in the flickering light of the screen Jesse's hand on Allisandra's breast.

He stands up. "Hey." He scoops up a few cubes of ice and pours more vodka in his cup.

"What?"

"I'll be back. Leave the window open."

"Why? You gonna listen? What are you, a perv?"

"Let the smoke out, dumbass."

Allisandra is keeping her eyes on Gus, shining like an invitation. If he had wanted a fight, it would have already started. "Twenty minutes. I'll be back."

The white paint of the stairwell is fresh and bright. The darkness outside feels welcoming. Small can lights shine along the sidewalk; the air is warm and loud. A home style restaurant once stood between Shadeland Avenue and the hotel, which sits back a hundred yards from the street. All that's left of the diner is gravel and pilings. As he approaches the edge of the parking lot, his eyes adjust to the darkness and details emerge, clumps of thick weeds, chunks of concrete, the overhang of the leaning garage on the corner. He's never seen anyone open the doors. He doesn't know what's inside. He takes a short drink and sits down on a piling in the darkness, reaching for a cigarette.

Most of the lights in the hotel are off. Close to the building, the parking lot is full. A night bug screeches out from the trees, a buzzing cycle that catches his train of thought. When a car turns into the Meridian's lot, he watches it without moving.

He sits for what seems like a long time, sipping the vodka until it's gone, thinking of nothing because there's nothing to think, his mind as empty as the air through which he reaches up and scratches his shoulder. Each particle of time elongates, releasing with the cars when the red lights turn green. If it felt like anything, it felt like dissolving. He is part of the traffic. He is the concrete piling. He is an empty plastic cup.

Slowly, beneath the indistinct night rush, appears a contradictory sound, a bass thump that can only be music. The sound stops when a car pulls in. It starts again when it leaves. He sits forward, turning his head to listen. Far down the row of cars, tail lights flash on and off unexpectedly. Someone must be leaving. He waits for the engine to turn over. Instead, the lights flash on and off again, a dark van next to a Lincoln.

He drops the plastic cup to the ground and stomps

it. He stands up, shifting into his clothes. The dead cell phone bumps in his pocket. The music stops and a car door slams. Even from a distance, he can tell she's a girl, walking toward him in silhouette with swinging steps and long hair flying up at her shoulders. Why she is flip-flopping toward the dark corner of the parking lot is a mystery. She stops six cars away, puts her hands on her hips and says, "Hey."

In the dark, he can't see her all that well. "Hey, who? Hey, me?"

"I saw you walk across the parking lot, and then I saw your cigarette."

Her voice is different, the sound of her Os, as if they're broken in the middle. "What did you see?"

"I just told you, your cigarette. This hotel is shit. I can't believe my mother is making us stay here in one room with all my cousins."

The girl looks too young, she looks like trouble. He has to go back upstairs. He has two sisters, younger, at home. "That's okay. You should listen to your mom."

"Why, where are you going?"

He laughs. "Hell if I know."

"Hey," she says, suddenly closer without seeming to move her feet, "do you want to walk to the store?"

"No." He shakes his head. He doesn't spend money at the stores on Shadeland when he can go to the Catch-n-Go eight blocks away where they sell Coke, two cans for a dollar. Standing closer, she's up to his shoulder, her hair smelling sweet like flowers, not the kind he used to pick, something like oranges or lemons.

A car turns into the parking lot. The girl cries out and ducks. Gus follows her example, hits the piling with his leg, falls to the gravel where he sprawls on its sharp pebbles. He flips onto his back and moans out loud. Like landing on a bed of nails.

"Hey, are you okay? Where are you?" The girl separates from the darkness and nudges him with her shoe. She kneels down, her hand finding his leg just above the knee. "Did you break anything?"

The weight of her hand, the warmth of her hand. He could almost fall asleep. The weight and warmth travel to the pit of his stomach and then circle downward. "I'm okay," he says, thinking he must sit up but unable to break the spell. At least in the dark, she can't see how her hand is making him hard.

"Great. If I had to call 911, I don't even know your name. I'd have to say, some guy in the parking lot fell down. I think he broke his leg."

The dark sky swims with thin clouds marbled faintly orange and brown around vast islands of black space where a few stars manage to shine through. He feels the warmth of her hand and pretends he's somewhere clean and soft, a bed in the clouds with white sheets.

"Hey," she says, squeezing until the muscles jump in his leg. She stands up. "I'm Cara. What's your name?"

"Gus." He brushes dust from his hands and jeans, sits up and props his hands on his knees. "I have to go back with my friends."

"Where are they? Are you staying at the hotel?"

"Something like that."

"Can I come? The parking lot is boring."

What would it hurt, they weren't staying long. The party was almost over. "Okay, help me up." When he holds out his hand, he knows that she'll take it. He knows that she'll follow him in.

Room 112

At ten o'clock, once he'd swallowed his night pills and injected insulin, Horace Benford crawled into bed. The hotel was nothing special; he had stayed in hundreds, maybe thousands, on business trips, not to count the vacations. His room had the same particle board furniture, average mattress and amenities (coffee pot, hair dryer, TV, clock radio, little soaps and shampoos) standard to any lower, mid-priced joint. All he needed was a roof, clean sheets, and hot water to shave in the morning, decent air conditioning to sleep, a bedside lamp for a night light, and a working TV with cable. He turned off CNN and pulled back the covers before lowering his stiff, heavy body. The surgery to remove veins from his legs had left him with numb spots that tingled, radiant sensations like his calf was asleep or like he had banged his shin, wood meeting bone in blank awareness.

When his back hit the mattress, his joints released, letting go their cramped upright grip to ache in a different way. He propped his feet up on the folded down bedspread. The nurse had showed him how to press a finger to his leg and feel afterwards for depressions. Driving long distances caused him to retain water. His dry, discolored skin held a shallow crater, but it wasn't the worst he had seen. Leaving his feet up would drain the water. Mentally, he told Dorothy it wasn't a problem. If he hadn't wanted to drive to bring flowers to her grave, he would have stayed home in Tinley Park. Linda, their daughter, thought the trip was too much; she said because of his arrhythmia and diabetes, but she didn't volunteer to drive him, so what was she good for? The only obstacles he ran into were road hogs crowding the left lane; he'd laid on the horn, and then laid off. Dorothy had hated his honking. If she was alive, he would have stopped for good, but she wasn't, and idiots remained, at least forty percent of the general driving population, he figured.

Sitting up strained his lower back. He put down his elbows to lower his head. Sometimes it felt like Dorothy was alive, had only gone on a vacation, and would be back tomorrow or the next day at latest. Other days, it felt like she'd been gone forever. Their house had grown dingy over the past two years. Dust collected in all the corners. He changed the furnace filter, but it didn't change one damn thing. Nothing was hunky-dory. Dammit, he was supposed to die first. They'd talked about it for years. When he said, "You'll be married before I'm in the ground," she turned flustery mad and said, "I don't even want the first man I married, why would I want a second one?"

He chuckled out loud. He could always get her goat, even if he couldn't change her mind. That was Dorothy, mad as an old wet hen even when she was a spring chicken.

He shouldn't have argued with her in the end when the tumor pressed against her eye. She wore a black eye patch beneath her puff of white hair like a dandelion gone-to-seed. She said, "I've decided I want to be buried with my family down by Boggstown." In her flowered house dress, she looked like an old woman pirate. He'd argued, "Why so far away? I thought I was your family." It was more than a hop-skip-and-jump to Boggstown; it was close to two hundred miles.

But she meant family in her own sense: grandmothers, mother and father, a brother and sister, uncle, aunts. She named off her dead family in Boggstown until he got tired of listening, even the youngest dead, an aunt who died at birth and had a rosebud carved on her tombstone. Dorothy raised her heart-shaped chin and adjusted the fit of her eye patch. "There'll always be somebody to put flowers on my grave there. Family always visits." She accused him, "If I'm buried here, you'll never bring flowers. They might cost more than a nickel." And then she added, "After you and Linda are gone, who's left to bring flowers, anyway?"

He'd informed her there was a thing called perpetual flower service, but she said it wouldn't be the same. "People hired for money to put flowers over my dead body," she snorted. "Do you know how much that costs?"

He didn't, and money was one of their differences, which Dorothy knew and used against him. He never spent where he shouldn't have spent. He never bought other women jewelry, roses, or champagne. His paycheck came home and Dorothy managed the money, except for bonuses and savings. She called him stingy, but she was no spendthrift. When the women at the club started wearing furs, Dorothy stayed with brushed black wool. She said, "Mink's so heavy. It's like wearing upholstery.

It makes me feel like a walking sofa."

She had been a walking sofa, all right, all one-hundred-and-ten pounds of her. His beloved wife, his beloved Dorothy, deserved to be buried exactly where she wanted. She was laid to rest in Boggstown in the plot of an infertile aunt, whose long-dead husband had purchased half-a-dozen in advance of children that never happened. Other relatives had taken some spots, but two places remained. When Horace said he'd rather be dead than buried next to her cousin, Dorothy said, "You're too mean to die. You'll live to be a hundred and the world no better for it."

When she said it, he knew it was true: a premonition arose within him that she would be the first to die. He couldn't bear it. He went outside to water the tomatoes that hadn't yet started to flower. By the time tomatoes came on the vine, she was buried and Horace was alone.

When a family member offered the other grave spot in Boggstown to their Linda, they discovered she already had plans. She came to Tinley Park every weekend at the end, when Dorothy's cancer was bad. Sitting together, they looked like the mouse and the elephant: mother, white-haired, no bigger than a thumb sketch, daughter, twice her size with thinning brown hair and thick ankles.

Horace wasn't so surprised that their daughter went and made plans to bury herself. She decided to be buried in a cemetery in Elgin, where she taught school for twenty-seven years. She never accused them directly, but he and Dorothy knew how she felt, that they had ruined her life by forbidding her to marry a man from India when she was in college. It was not that they personally disliked Raj, but mixing wasn't done back then. It would have been too hard on the children. Instead, they encouraged her to marry a man from western Illinois, Larry Wirth, who turned out to be an alcoholic. When Linda got a divorce, it was the first in the family, which made it doubly bitter for all of them.

No matter if Linda blamed them, Horace held her solely responsible, not counting Larry who had moved away to Ohio not long after. When people vowed marriage for life, the bargain had been struck. He could not have imagined being anything other than married to Dorothy until the very end. A marriage made a marriage was a marriage forever. He'd brought three floral arrangements for her grave with lavender, red and yellow, silk gladiolas, carnations and roses. He wanted to show her that he could let go of a nickel. She'd had definite opinions about flowers and housework, bridge and burials, budgets and husbands.

If he had been a different man, he would have loved Dorothy differently but he couldn't have loved her more. She'd known that. She had to know. No matter when other women came around, he always came home to Dorothy. In the early years, she cried and caused scenes because she didn't understand that men had needs, and he was a man; she wouldn't have married him, otherwise. One night, she opened the bedroom window and threw all his suits and shirts on the lawn. It was just after they moved into the big house and turned the little house into a garage. Dorothy went hysterical, ripping clothes from the closet and shouting until she woke up Linda. While she went to take care of their screaming daughter, he gathered his clothes in the dark, furious, steamed as a hot poker, glad it was the middle of the night.

The next morning, he packed a suitcase and said he was going out of town on business. He didn't tell her where, or when he'd be back. When he finally returned three days later, Dorothy wasn't speaking but they managed to patch things up. It wasn't easy, but they got through it. That was what he wished that Linda had time to learn, to take the good and the bad. Dorothy could only be mad at him for so long, and then her heart would soften. It was what he loved about his wife. It was one of the things he loved most.

In the months after she died, pains started in his chest. He had believed it was heart burn or his heart breaking, a severe and physical disturbance. He'd once gone for a while with a hippy-type who talked about New Age bullshit: zodiac signs, auras, fortune telling, prophecy mumbo-jumbo. The only thing she'd ever said that made any sense was about a connection between the mind and the body. She said when sadness settled in an organ, it festered and caused real pain. When he felt his heart, he could only think of Dorothy. Then one day a sharpness stole his breath away, and he had to sit down in the grocery store, letting go of the cart in the cereal aisle and sinking to the floor. The manager called an ambulance that came and took him away, sirens, red lights, the whole caboose. The surgeon in the emergency room said Horace had multiple blockages, heart disease; she planned to do a triple bypass the next morning.

The only person he could think to contact was Linda. His old friend Norm couldn't drive any more because of cataracts. Horace was all doped up, but he still knew that Dorothy wasn't with him. It was Linda, their daughter, who picked him up six weeks later at the convalescence center and drove him home to Tinley Park.

In his first moments home after surgical rehab, he lay back in his recliner, feeling bruised as a fallen peach, looking out the back window across the unmowed lawn at the blowsy tree line by the old drainage ditch. The surgery had left him uncertain; he lost time, could not remember days, scenes arriving through screens of morphine and sleep, time afterwards marked by sitting up because otherwise he couldn't breath, his chest sore, the wound still damp, breastbone wired together. Linda went through the house, opening curtains and blinds. She unpacked a grocery bag, putting away easy foods like soup, bread, eggs, cheese, and crackers.

When she finished, she came into the den and sat down on the corduroy couch. "How do you feel?"

He felt like he'd been beaten up in an alley; that was what the surgeon said he would feel like. "I've been better, but I think I'll survive. You go on home when you need to."

"I think we need to talk about a long-term plan. I can't drive down every week from Elgin."

Their daughter looked large and stubborn, her arms crossed over her stomach. He shouldn't have expected more out of Linda. He said, "Don't bother talking about the house. I don't ever plan on selling."

If she was so worried about driving, she could keep herself in Elgin. A visiting nurse had been scheduled to stop by the house every other day. The hospital arranged a temporary cleaning lady. The house he built with his own hands was more than a piece of real estate. He built the "little" house first, sixty years ago, during the Second World War, when no one could get supplies, but he had connections; thinking of a certain load of two-by-fours always made him smile. He built the "big" house later, after the War, and converted the little house into a two-car garage. Both were level with the ground, no steps to trip on, with radiant heat embedded in the floor. He connected the two buildings with a covered walk, and eventually enclosed the space to build a trapezoid den with wide windows front and back and a fireplace against the garage wall. That house was his life with Dorothy, every chair, sofa, table, every curtain, down to the moldings that she had used for plate racks.

How could Linda possibly understand? She'd thrown away her marriage, didn't know that if you knocked around in a marriage, everyone stood back up in the end. It was like the silly idea Dorothy held onto that he'd always wanted a son. She'd said, "That's why you run around, because I can't have more children. It's not fair, Horace. It's not my fault."

He didn't give a good goddamn about a son, but he could never convince his wife. From what he'd seen of children, including their own daughter, ingratitude was the primary trait. He'd heard stories from other men of children who stole things, sons who wouldn't work, sons who drank too much and took to drugs, daughters who went on the streets. When he was boy, he was thankful to his parents for anything they could provide, a warm bed, food on the table, a pair of shoes once a year.

Children had changed for the worse during his lifetime, though Linda understood her obligations. She came to see him a few times after the surgery, driving down on the weekend. When she visited the house at Tinley Park, she read or did paperwork at the dining room table while he watched baseball or walked in the yard. In August, the cherry tree in the backyard fruited. He showed her the ladder and the curved basket that strapped around your waist, but she didn't want to pick them, perfectly good cherries. He couldn't lift his arms above his chest yet. A year's worth of cherries gone to waste, to the birds, drawing wasps on the ground.

The nightstand lamp that he left lit in honor of Dorothy

glowed red behind his lids, flashing and coiling in paisley spirals, and he saw himself gathering cherries this August, stepping to the top rung of the ladder, reaching high for clustered stems, the dimpled fruit soft as miniature plums. When they were young, Dorothy would help him stone them, make cherry cobbler, and whiskey sours thick with fruit to soak up the liquor. On late summer nights, they sat in the backyard and looked up at patterns of stars. All the old crowd, Norm and Sandy, Ronald and Kay, the Lieutenant, Don Graham and his girl. They played the stereo and danced on the lawn, Dorothy small in his arms. She used to step on his feet when she wanted attention. He danced his wife around, smelling her perfume, touching lightly her fine-boned spine, so petite he could lift her in the air without even trying. When she wanted to see him, she had to look up and her lips were slightly open. She had been beautiful, and he had been handsome; together, they had been something.

A resounding boom opened Horace's eyes. It came like thunder from above. He blinked at the room's ceiling, but it didn't crack. He lived in anticipation of apocalypse, the day when society finally went mad. All the news on TV about bombings and guns, people shooting up soldiers and schools, missing victims, mass murders, machetes, beheadings, and mutilations. Running airplanes into skyscrapers. Any idiot could fight a bad, cheap war. If the U.S. had any sense, it would bomb its enemies into glass; bomb them until they were bouncing rubble. In his day, the country had some pride. After Viet Nam, things went to the dung hill.

He waited for a second crash, his heart thumping against scarred muscles. A wave of indigestion competed for his discomfort, along with the urge to urinate. He leaned forward to check his leg. He decided not to call the front desk unless the noise happened again. The authorities nowadays weren't worth a bent, half-penny nail. In his day, you didn't even have to lock your car, but if it did get stolen, the cops actually cared. They'd come to your house to take the report. They'd send out an APB.

He hauled himself out of bed, drooping jockey shorts, and clomped to the bathroom to get rid of water. He held the toilet seat against the tank and leaned forward to do his business, slipping his penis from the leg of his shorts. Dorothy called his penis his thing, as in, "Keep that thing away from me." She'd always been a lady in the sack, unlike some of the others. The last woman Horace had been with, he hadn't particularly liked. She was too tall and coarse, make-up caked on a large-pored face. In bed, she said, "Hurry up," and he had to pretend to finish.

He couldn't recall her name. He could hardly remember any of their names, though at one point he counted their faces and got up to fifty-eight. He tended to remember specific moments: dancing with the brunette at Reunion Tower; the fake blonde with nipples pink as lipstick; the next-door-type who refused to get on top. The time a husband had gotten involved. He remembered that one's name. Donna.

He had had a rule against married women, but she had been deceptive. She took off her ring; she mentioned an apartment. Her husband had known about the affair before Horace knew there was a husband. The man called him in his office at the plant, threatened to tell Dorothy everything if Horace didn't end things.

Discretion had always been part of their bargain. When Horace finally got hold of Donna, he called her what she was, a whore and a liar. She said, "Please, don't do this. You're not happy, either," but Horace's mind was made up. He quit the affair and sweated the days. Waiting for the communication that would give him away, he dreaded leaving for work and rushed home as soon as possible. Dorothy didn't know why he was there, but it made her happy. That year he'd painted the garage and latticed the patio. Donna's husband never called, but remembering still made Horace angry.

He flushed the toilet and left the bathroom. Back in the room, he pulled loose the spread, sheets and blanket, rearranging the pillows at the foot of the bed. It was one of Dorothy's tricks she'd come up with when she was going through the change. He used to think it was funny that a woman who all her life complained of being cold had night sweats that drenched her like buckets. He said, "Turning around in bed's not going to lower the temperature," but she insisted, "It really makes me feel cooler."

Turning around in bed didn't change the temperature, but on bad nights it comforted him. Crawling in backwards, he leaned toward the headboard and checked his legs again. The water was draining but not as fast as he wanted. He settled back on the pillows and belched his indigestion, holding his chest with both arms. He told Dorothy not to worry about it. Last year, he couldn't bring flowers to her grave because of the surgery. Next year, who knew if he'd still be alive? A marriage made a marriage was a marriage forever. Had they had rough spots? Yes, there had been those. But it took two to tango, two to dance when the cherries came in. Dorothy knew that. She had understood. He couldn't have loved her more.

⁘ Room 205 ⁘

In spite of her worries concerning her niece, Merry Mentweather closed her eyes. The bed wasn't that comfortable, like cardboard on top of cotton balls, but the room was cool and dark, throbbing with regular sound: the shush-shush of the air conditioner, the resting sighs of her daughters, the television turned sweet and low. She twisted her shoulder and rolled over on her stomach, settling her cheek against the scratchy pillow. She turned over thinking, I'll be up all night, and the next thing she didn't know, she was gone.

In the dream, she stood in blinding darkness with lightning and wind outside, the city hall of a tourist town leaning into its timbers, and all she knew was, it's too late. The door flew open and a black shadow rushed in, a creature like a flying, animated oil slick with black talons and hot charcoal eyes, sweeping like wind up the staircase because she hadn't locked the door. Upstairs, her niece huddled in a bed holding a strange golden-haired child that Merry didn't understand, in an old-fashioned dress, like a doll but alive. Cara, Cara's wide frightened eyes, pleading wordlessly for help, but Merry was too late getting down to the foyer—she couldn't see what was happening upstairs—and the wind swung the darkness round and round, spinning the old house with Merry inside it.

She startled awake, turning over. Heart pounding, she panted and sat up. Shadows flashed around the room, cast by the still-on TV. Her heart beat so loud she felt afraid its thumping might cause a heart attack. To calm herself, she breathed slowly and deeply, her hand pressed against her chest. It was a dream, nothing but a nightmare; but all of it had been so real.

The clock on the nightstand said eleven-fifty, the digital numbers made with reassuringly straight lines. She'd slept less than two hours. She touched the nightstand to steady herself, gaining from its sturdiness. It was the worst nightmare she'd ever experienced, like the oil creature was an immortal being, so horrible that no one had written it down, an evil impulse that existed and against which the world had forever been helpless. It was like being possessed by demons; the darkness of it too much. She bowed her head and prayed, seeking comfort in seeking God: *Please Lord, in your mercy, take away the dream and remind me of goodness, that You are the Light of the World.*

In the bathroom, she searched out a hand towel that wasn't too soggy and splashed cold water on her face, patting it dry and wondering that she rarely dreamed or remembered dreams any more, as if dreaming belonged to the young because her mind was too old and crowded. Most nights she fell exhausted into bed and sank into a sleep so deep that nothing touched her until the alarm went off. Nightmares, night terrors, she'd only had one or two; dreams she could barely remember, snarling wild dogs and nakedness. Not sleeping, insomnia, was more of a problem, waking up worried in the middle of the night, but that didn't happen often. She enjoyed her sleep. When the girls were babies, they never let her get any rest.

The mirror reflected her middle-aged face, its heavy cheeks and blotchy complexion. She touched the damp skin that would become her grandmother's jowl, remembering the time when she was young and a boy named Victor said she had perfect lips.

It was vain back then, it was vanity now. Merry ran a quick brush through her gray-flecked hair. It didn't matter what people looked like; what mattered was what was inside, though Genevieve would disagree. Her sister said if God didn't want women to be beautiful, He wouldn't have invented make-up, not that God made the make-up, but He made the scientists who made wrinkle cream. Her sister could twist words into a streak of logic that Merry couldn't untangle. She worried not only for Genevieve's soul but also for that of Cara. Since Merry was awake, she would have to check on her niece, who didn't know the meaning of Christ, much less self-respect or character. But mother and daughter were just alike: vain, willful and stubborn. Wild women supposedly ran in the family, but that was just an excuse. Who was their mother talking about, anyway; none of the aunts or cousins ran around with men or went to bars, only Genevieve and only because she could because she left home and didn't look back. She knew how to make her own way; she had never asked anybody for anything.

Until now. Genevieve was back in Pittsburgh with a daughter who insisted on camping out in parked cars. What was the golden-haired child in the dream? She wasn't innocent like Merry's girls; she seemed to have adult knowledge. Merry shuddered because the doll child was so freaky, and she didn't understand it.

She turned off the bathroom light. In the flickering darkness of the room, she sat gently on the bed to slip on her tennis shoes. Genevieve didn't move, the only evidence she was still alive her regular whispery breathing. She was no help, or Cara's father, either, a thousand miles away, probably out on the town with a Hooters' girl. At least, that was the last rumor they'd had of him. Some little, hot mama half his age.

Maybe Jimmy was no angel, but he never ran around on Merry, except for the once in Arkansas when he traveled selling satellite systems. If some other woman wanted Jimmy that bad, she could gladly take him, though it would leave the girls with an absent father. Anyway, Jimmy would never get a divorce; he felt so sorry for the affair that he cried and didn't drink for a month. He knew he had it good with Merry.

For the second time since ten o'clock, she opened Room 205's door and stepped into the hall.

After being in the dim, crowded room, the expanded space of the empty hallway made her feel large and somehow solid, collected in her own body. A wall sconce toward the exit stairs revealed a burned-out light bulb.

She walked in the other direction toward the ice machine alcove, trying to be extra quiet. Decent people were sleeping, regular people who didn't have a niece named Trouble. It must be nice to be Genevieve, the woman who never worried or only about unimportant things, like whether the restaurant had real silverware, or if her shoes made her ankles look slim, not about things that mattered, like why at thirty-nine-years-old she was on her second divorce and already thinking about men. It was true, both of Genevieve's ex-husbands had issues; at the very least, overbearing personalities. Cara's father, Don, had linebacker shoulders; he once broke a golf club in half against a tree at a course that cost more than one hundred dollars a round. In spite of the fact that both Genevieve's husbands were financially successful, you could never know a man until you married him. But better to live with the man you know than go looking for a different problem; like the song said, love the one you're with. Of course, Genevieve's marriages were really none of her business. No matter their differences, they were still sisters.

Someone had left an ice bucket lid lying on the sill by the ice machine. Merry looked past it to the parking lot. The van was still there, the blanket visible through the windshield. She didn't see anything moving. Had Cara crawled into the back seat to have more room to sleep? Maybe it was warm in the van, especially with the windows rolled up. If she got hot, it served her right. Merry couldn't see anything from the window. She was going to have to take a closer look. She decided to take the stairs down because the elevator was too noisy.

The same clerk, a young woman, glanced up from the front desk. Merry nodded and kept walking. What a struggle it must be to stay awake all night; she didn't think she could do it. She wondered if night workers ever dozed off. Her rubber soles squeaked on the tile.

Pushing out the lobby doors, she stepped through the vestibule and into the breezeway. Freeway sounds enveloped her, a loud flowing rush that actually moved air, cooler than she'd expected. She couldn't remember the last time she had been outside this late. She hadn't been a night owl in years, not since before she'd had the girls, and those late nights she regretted. She walked self-consciously to the van, checking out the shadows of the parking lot, aware that all the experts said the best defense was hyper-awareness. In spite of the constant traffic, Merry felt safe enough, though a woman could never be sure. The advice columns said to look alert;

don't look like a victim. She approached the van and peered inside, using her right hand as a visor.

When she didn't immediately see Cara, her heart double-jumped again. She circled twice, straining her eyes to the shadows, checking the floorboards and cargo space. The second time around, she tried all the doors and discovered the driver's side was open. Automatically, she checked beneath the floor mat and discovered the keys left behind. Did that mean Cara planned to come back? Or that she'd left for good, taken off hitch-hiking, or been taken, kidnapped against her will?

With the door of the van still open, Merry looked around the lot, quiet as far as she could see, parked cars, no one coming or going. Down the street, a convenience store flashed its sign, and further on a restaurant or bar; she thought she could read the word "Karaoke." There was traffic on the main street, not a lot, but steady. The scene revealed no signs of a struggle. The van held no other clues. She rummaged around, looking for a note that turned out to be nonexistent. Girls like Cara didn't worry about notes. The blanket didn't look disturbed. A car pulled into the Meridian and another pulled out, driven by a woman talking on her cell. Merry pocketed the keys, locked the van's door, and slammed it.

She bowed her head and prayed for Cara's safety: *Dear God, protect her wherever she's at*; then she opened her eyes and headed in to check at the front desk. Maybe someone had seen her niece, maybe she went inside to the lady's room. Squeaking her way across the tiles, the clerk heard and looked up. "Excuse me," Merry said, "I have a problem. I think my niece is missing. I was wondering if you'd seen her?"

Room 212

When the tall man and his wife packed up and left, they left on all the lights. Someone had slept in both beds, or at least pulled down the bedspreads and rumpled the sheets. Both chairs at the table had been sat in. A dresser drawer was pulled out. All the lampshades were tilted at crooked angles. The carpet was dented all over, like the maid moved the furniture every day. The air conditioner ran full blast. The temperature was freezing.

Monica LeMaire put her suitcase on the nearest bed and surveyed the room. What kind of people made such a mess? She pushed the lampshades back to level, closed the drawers, and turned off the A.C. She checked the sheets of the bed farthest from the door. It looked slightly less lived in. She tossed the pillows and fluffed them up. The phone started to ring.

"Good evening," Duncan said, "this is a courtesy call

from the front desk. How did you find the room?"

"It was messy, but I'm straightening up. The air conditioner works."

"That's good to know. If you have any problems, feel free to call."

Monica hung up and sat down on the bed, its commercial coils resisting. The phone on the nightstand looked so plastic and worthless. She was free, but she wasn't getting married. Ivan just wasn't right; like swimming was criminal behavior, like missing *Law and Order* was a tragedy. He could be impossible. Not that the loss of her wedding wasn't going to be difficult. She blinked, sniffing hard. But she couldn't marry a man who blamed her without warning whenever the unexpected happened. She couldn't imagine if Stan had drowned. The thought was too horrific, a near-miss obliteration of her life's fabric even larger than walking out on Ivan. Sitting alone, exhausted, on the bed in the messed-up hotel room, Monica broke down and sobbed.

Loud and clear, the crying echoed back. She heard it and looked around. The room had the same low boxy ceiling as the room she'd shared with Stan and Ivan, the same fire detector and sprinkler heads, nothing especially acoustical about it. "Hello?" she called. No echo appeared. She'd probably just imagined it. Her face felt swollen from holding everything in. She was going to get a sinus infection. What kind of woman walked out on her fiancé and his little boy? Monica inhaled in a series of quivers. All she had ever wanted was love, the kind that came with a family. But the men were never right, or she should have married younger when the future had seemed long and bright, so open that she couldn't imagine not waiting until the perfect man appeared. And then he hadn't. And then there was Ivan. What was she left with now?

The sound of her sobs came back like echoes, the chimes of a distant bell, her crying trapped somehow by the walls. The echo was like sad music, but it also sounded like mocking. It only stopped when she stopped. She stood up to open the window so the air could circulate better. An Indianapolis *Yellow Pages*, big as a boot box, lay in the middle of the floor. She stepped over it, wondering how she had missed it earlier. But she shouldn't judge a gift room by its messiness. Look how much money she'd saved, and she was going to need every penny to pay off the nonrefundable wedding deposits. It had been going to be a storybook affair, her colors violet and ivy green.

Monica unlatched the window, which didn't have any screen, and slid it open. Outside, the world was a warm dark space marked by pools of light that shimmered and raced when the traffic lights changed. It looked like a movie of a city, a complete waste of night, the stars blocked out by light pollution and exhaust. Wires drooped from an endless field of poles, buildings crowded together, and stunted, little trees grew in the spaces in between.

They joked in Wooster that a traffic jam was five cars stuck at a red light. She could have married Tommy Young after high school, but she would have had to move to Cincinnati. A car turned into the parking lot. She realized how it must look, a woman leaning out of a well-lit window.

Monica pulled the left curtain half-shut. There were too many people in cities, too many people and too close together. She suddenly thought of her mother, but it was too late to call, and besides, what would she say? She couldn't count on her mother to show unconditional sympathy. A mother's philosophy shouldn't be, "In life, everyone has problems." For her, Ivan was a good man, and Stan a bonus grandchild. She wanted her daughter to be happy, had said more than once, "This is what you've always wanted, make the most of it." She was beading the union candle by hand for the ceremony.

Monica picked up the phone book and set it on the dresser next to the TV. Most of the time, her heart was undetectable, beating regularly in her chest. What spun her in every direction was what went on in her head. She knew all along she'd been settling, trying to overlook the ways that Ivan annoyed her. He could be overly congenial; he pretended too hard to like things when he didn't, and then he overreacted. Why had she let it go on so long? What would Stan grow up thinking of women, first his mother disappearing, and then his mother figure when he was barely four years old? Not that she hadn't tried to avoid that; she never let him call her "Mama." Monica stripped off the t-shirt and shorts she'd thrown on over her pajamas and fished her toothbrush out of her suitcase.

Ivan always wanted to talk all night, tell her stories of his life, some of them interesting but they went on too long; he'd still be talking when they only had a few minutes before she had to drive home. "Hush," she'd say, cuddling into his arms; then, pointblank, "Please, shut up." She didn't mean to hurt his feelings, but they had years ahead of them for talking. When he told her about the time he was a boy and the school bus swerved and went in a ditch because a cow ran across the road, she thought of the time on the school bus when a girl spit in her hair, but she didn't mention it. The spitting girl was more an incident than story, a distinction that would benefit Ivan.

Room 212's bathroom, unlike the bedroom, was spotless, the towels undisturbed on the chrome shelves, the sink and shower shining. Monica brushed her teeth and washed her face, patted it dry with a towel. She crawled into the bed with the least rumpled sheets and turned off the light. She had been a good sleeper since she was a baby, according to her mother, but the mattress didn't feel right. She tossed and turned, feeling lonely. The pillows were flat and hard. She kept thinking of Stan, how pitiful and cold he looked dripping against Ivan's wet shirt. He was like a funny little miracle, his sturdy legs nothing but muscles because he was always jumping. He didn't mention his mother as often, a good thing since she didn't bother to keep in touch. But he was four years old. He needed someone, and Ivan was next to useless.

Stan hadn't even known what a firefly was; how to catch them with cupped hands and slip them into a canning jar to make a firefly lantern. Ivan was more likely to turn a summer evening in the yard into a lecture on electricity, how it flowed through wires like water flowed through pipes. She wanted to go with the imagery, but at the end, the electricity leaped from the socket like water rushing from a pipe, and she said, "A leaky faucet has never electrocuted anyone."

Ivan laughed, but he had no faith; he was insecure in ways she couldn't fathom. Why did he care that she liked to do her own laundry? Or when she locked the bathroom door? Why did he expect her to enjoy going to the hardware store to look at screws, and when she said she wanted to stay home and read, he made out like it was a personal insult?

Not that she was perfect. And he'd wanted to have a baby. She'd told him about the name Lily, a dream daughter once more deferred, Lily with the fluffy blonde hair, a baby girl to be a sister for Stan.

As soon as Monica cried, she startled awake, the echo as loud as before in spite of the open window and the traffic noise. She sat up in bed and turned on the lamp. It was three minutes to midnight. The room looked messier than before, a pile of tissues crumpled in the corner, the ice bucket lying on its side. The echo was jolting, like the dream of taking an accidental step off a cliff. She'd seen documentaries of haunted houses and ghosts, but she'd never actually had an experience. Was the echo the sound of a ghost? Is that why the tall man left? Monica's motto had always been: What you don't believe in can't hurt you.

The walls of the room seemed to bow in slightly. If only Ivan could take a look at them. He knew everything about buildings; she trusted his knowledge of construction, even if he was impossible to live with. The phone on the nightstand had easy room-to-room calling. A breeze ruffled the curtains inward; the flutter made her jump. She picked up the receiver and dialed Room 170.

Ivan answered sounding groggy. "Hello? What? Hello?"

His voice didn't reassure her. "Ivan, are you awake?"

"Monica? Monica, where are you? I'm sorry."

She hadn't meant to get him excited. She said, "Ivan, I need to ask you a question about the room I'm in."

"Whatever it is, the answer's yes."

"Listen, will you? Something's strange. This room has an echo." She looked around at the messiness. Had the other bedspread been pulled that far back? Had the chairs at the table moved? It was impossible to tell with all the dents in the carpet.

"I don't know. Is one of the walls angled? Do they seem excessively rigid? Say something and let me hear it."

She couldn't confess that she'd been crying; he'd take it as positive feeling. "It's not like that. I can't make it happen, Ivan."

"How do you know it's an echo, then?"

At that moment, the phone book slid off the dresser and landed with a thump on the floor. Monica jumped and screamed, standing straight up in the bed.

"What is it? What's going on?"

"This room," she said. "The phone book fell off the dresser. The pillows feel like rocks. When I cry, it echoes, and it's driving me crazy. The man said that it was haunted, but I didn't believe him."

"Man? What man? What man, Monica?"

She was trapped in concentric circles of irrational experience and disbelief, the hard reality of the phone book's location, the absence of motive for what moved it, the inexplicable echo, the dented carpet, her recently broken engagement, the implacable impulse to leap from the mattress and flee while she still had time, owned her life, her wits, the same impulse to run that delivered her to this crazy room to begin with.

"Monica," Ivan demanded. "Say something. Tell me what's going on."

She looked around the room. Even though nothing was moving, all the furniture felt poised for motion. Then she saw the chair. It had been facing the window. Now the seat faced the door. Something or someone hovered near it, invisible. She could feel a malevolent force.

"Don't hurt me, don't hurt me." She dropped the phone.

"Where are you? Monica, I'm coming."

But she'd already leaped off the bed. She didn't care if she had her toothbrush, or that she was wearing pajamas. She grabbed her purse, her shoes, and jammed the suitcase zipper closed before running out of the room, the bag's heaviness flinging her arm. The door opened more than easily, but she bruised herself against its frame, propelled by the feel of air panting behind her. When the door shut, a booming slam reverberated.

She ran down the hall toward the lobby, toward the solidity of real people, the walls of the hall tilting and righting in her senses. Panic drove her, a galvanizing sense that didn't leave at the corner. Terrified, she turned and looked back. The hall glowed a placid gold above deep burgundy carpet minus one burned out light. Whatever was in the room didn't seem to have followed her.

She rolled her shoulders, shaking, and told herself to breathe. All she had to do was walk down the stairs and through the lobby and find Stan and Ivan. There was no question that's what she'd do. Then they were packing up and leaving. She had to get out of this hotel; she could not stay here one second longer. The elevator was too slow. She jabbed at the button, but the doors didn't open.

Elaine looked up from the front desk as Monica fled, dragging her suitcase down the stairs. Should she go tell her about the room? But, no, what was the point? The manager would come out and she didn't want to deal with him. No, she needed to hurry. She could tell he didn't believe in ghosts. She only knew the phone book had fallen with nobody there to push it. All she wanted was to get back to Ivan and Stan, pack their bags and drive away. There was no point in pretending that anything was all right. She never wanted to see this hotel again. She reached the bottom of the stairs and turned left.

Ivan walked toward her from the back hall, a sleepy Stan yawning in his arms. When the boy saw her, he pointed and shouted, "Monica!"

Front Lobby

As soon as it was feasible, Duncan vacated the front desk to retreat to the manager's office for his lunch break. Normally he would have had an hour, but he promised Elaine that he'd hurry. He sat hunched at his desk, thoroughly enjoying his sandwich. Two bites of pumpernickel, spicy brown mustard and pastrami, followed by a snap of warm pickle, washed down with coffee moderately hot, heavy cream, no sugar. Propped open before him on the desk he shared with Henry, the assistant who worked alternating nights, was Volume 8 of the 1968 edition of the *Merit Students Encyclopedia*, a book he'd pulled from the Lost and Found.

He chewed his sandwich and contemplated an entry in the volume's approximate middle. It was a primitive pencil and charcoal rendering of two giant ground sloths in a wooded habitat. They looked like regular sloths, only hairier and bigger, verging on prehistoric, though the beasts survived late into the 16th century, migrating from South America to North. They were probably still lumbering around when Vazquez showed up to plunder what would become the American "South." There had to have been contact between Western man and animal, if Duncan, unlike the English at the time, granted the Spaniards to be human. The encyclopedia said ground sloths grew to be up to twenty feet. They could stand on their hind legs and pull down huge branches, like the Seminole legend of Tall Man. What if the giant ground sloth was the ancestor of the modern Big Foot? No wonder the creatures were most often seen by illiterates in remote, swampy forests. In the modern age, big, hairy, intelligent animals would have no choice but to go into hiding. Look what civilization did to the dolphins: sensitive mammals trapped in pools of water, forced to swim with tourists for dead fish.

Duncan reached the end of his pickle and poured another half-cup of coffee before flipping on through the volume. Given encyclopedias as a genre, the *Merit Students* 1968 series was superior, its information broad and deep, illustrated and detailed with drawings, photographs, reproductions, graphs, and overlays. It was bound in dark green leatherette textured like lizard skin, weighty and embossed in gold. Whoever went off and left Volume 8 had to regret it. If it was Duncan's book, he would have retrieved it, or not traveled with it in the first place. His theory was, don't travel with anything you care about losing. Not that he'd traveled extensively; only twice out of Indiana, once to D.C. on a class trip senior year and once to Vegas for a wedding. That had been the waste of the price of a tux. The marriage hardly lasted longer than the length of William Henry Harrison's presidency.

Thumbing through, Duncan stopped on a photograph given a quarter-page. Warren G. Harding, another past President, not much better than Harrison. The former president looked unhappy in the picture, like maybe he had a toothache, an unsmiling man with a sculpted jaw whose white hair clashed with jet black eyebrows. Harding's motto had been, "Return to normalcy," which meant politics as usual: a cabinet plagued by nepotism, vice, and corruption. A kindler, gentler history would remember Harding as a victim of his own soft nature, too collegial and trusting for the nation's own good. The president literally sickened to death when his administration fell to scandal. He spoke often afterwards to Hoover and others about the sad position of a man betrayed by those he trusted.

Did Duncan have to feel sorry for a guy like Harding, or just tell him, "Look, wake up and smell the asphalt. If you get elected to be leader of the wealthiest nation in history, have opinions and be ready to fight; stop whining that everyone's not as good and nice as you are." Maybe Harding wasn't the worst dead president, but he was nowhere near the most excellent, who was, in Duncan's opinion, Harry S. Truman, the famous Missourian who said, "The buck stops here."

On the next page, a picture showed Harding leaning over a balcony, sickly, faded, and thin. At least he had the fortitude not to leap to his death in front of an audience. Duncan was reading the details of the Teapot Dome Scandal when Elaine burst through the door. "Hey," he reminded her, "I said half-an-hour." They'd already discussed the fact that she needed to go home as soon as was humanly possible. All he wanted was a half-hour for lunch and now she'd interrupted it.

"Listen, Duncan, we have a different problem. This woman says her niece is missing."

"Missing in what way?"

"Missing, as in she went out to the parking lot and

never came back in."

"When?"

"Around ten o'clock."

"That was two hours ago."

"I don't know," Elaine shrugged. "Her name's Merry Mentwether. I told her I'd get the manager. She said it's Merry, like in Christmas." Elaine started to go. "And by the way, your red-headed girlfriend? She's not in 212, anymore. She came down the stairs in her pajamas and dragging a suitcase. This guy with a kid met her from the back wing."

"Right now?"

"A few minutes ago. Right after you shut the door and said not to disturb you." Elaine crossed her arms.

"Tell Merry like Christmas I'll be right there." He refused to acknowledge Elaine's attitude. The ex-bride must have gone back to her groom. Which one of them owned the kid? He wondered if something was really wrong with 212. As soon as he had a chance, he'd call Housekeeping, but first the missing girl. He didn't like nights when complications multiplied; it reminded him too much of math.

Merry Mentwether grew exponentially excited as she explained the situation. The room was registered in her sister's name, Genevieve currently Dawson, though she was changing her name back to Baker. Apparently Mentwether had three daughters of her own, all asleep where they should be in Room 205. Cara, the missing girl, was fifteen, last seen wearing pink shorts and a blue t-shirt. "She went to the van around ten," Mentwether said, pointing to her wrist.

"That's what I told him," Elaine put in.

Mentwether's voice was girlish, though she had to be forty. Duncan tried to understand. He asked, "And when did she come back in?"

The woman bit her dry bottom lip. Straight brown hair flattened against her head, a few coiling gray hairs sticking up, framing a face as soft and comfortable as an old pillow. "She didn't come in. That's what I'm saying. Genevieve said she could sleep in the van, but now she's not there." Mentwether nodded toward the parking lot.

A green Saturn pulled into the entry bay. A thin woman of medium height wearing a skirt, blouse and high heels got out and slammed the door at the same time that the driver exited. He wore a plaid button down and his hair was messed up. They met on the far side of the vehicle.

Duncan could only wish that Merry Mentwether were

twenty years younger and shaped more like the ex-bride, but dark, a brunette, though who was he kidding? Every woman he fantasized about turned into Marian. "And what does her mother say about all this?"

"Call your niece's cell," Elaine suggested.

"She doesn't have one, they just moved back to Pitt. Genevieve's asleep, but I'm going to wake her up, you can bet your last dollar on that."

Duncan felt thankful he wasn't Genevieve. Mentwether seemed a formidable lady, the kind who'd slice through obstacles with the steely versatility of a Swiss pocket knife, or machete hack her way out of a corn maze. "Yes, wake Genevieve up. That sounds like a good idea. Elaine, did you check with Housekeeping and Maintenance?"

"Clyde didn't answer, but I left a message. You want me to try again?"

"Have you started running the movie report?"

"I thought you were going to do that."

Mentwether's forehead creased in worried folds like the shape of concentric bell curves. "I don't know how much to worry. How worried would you be? If she were your niece, how much would you worry?"

Duncan's family, himself and two older sisters, were

all the family they had left. It didn't seem likely that any one of them would generate nieces or nephews. Neither of his sisters had reproduced. He himself actively avoided procreation, though he didn't mind practicing the motions when a willing partner appeared, a situation that happened at very infrequent intervals. "I can't say how worried I'd be. How worried are you?"

"I'd be worried," Elaine put in. "Plenty of crazies out there. You never know what the crazies will do."

"Thank you," Mentwether exhaled, obviously validated. "It's not my niece that worries me. It's the crazies and molesters."

The couple outside embraced in a kiss that didn't seem to have a limit. Get a room, Duncan thought, ha, ha. "If you believe your niece is in danger, it's one thing. But if you think she's just wandered off, I'd wait a while, look around. You know how teenagers are. Maybe start with the hallways."

"What hallways?"

Elaine answered, gesturing like an air steward indicating the plane's exits. "There are upper and lower halls to your right and left. At the end of each is a stairwell. Does she have a keycard? Otherwise she couldn't operate the remote entrances."

Mentwether looked toward the front and back wings, exposing the frizzy back of her head. “I don’t know, she had her purse with her.”

The kissing couple came into the lobby. She was more nervous than he was, tucking in her blouse, looking at the floor. The guy looked smitten, maybe smarmy, satisfied before the fact, not even worried about the lipstick smeared across his cheek.

Elaine ignored them in favor of Merry. “Is there anything I can do to help?”

Merry nodded sincerely. “Thanks, but not yet. I’m going to wake my sister up first.”

“Great plan. I bet your niece will show up. Don’t forget to check the halls.” Duncan appreciated the fact that Mentwether hadn’t accepted Elaine’s offer of assistance. He still had a quarter of his sandwich left. If he knew teenagers, and he had once been one, albeit a know-it-all, horny loser who wore his priapic desperation like a Templar shield, then he knew teenagers were prone to taking off and returning when you least expected them. Once he sneaked away from swimming at church camp to hide in the bushes beside the girls’ shower house, where he had a handy time listening to the squeals and giggles of naked girls soaping their bodies.

The smitten man stepped up to the desk. "Good evening, or maybe it's good morning. Either way, I need a room."

Duncan said, "We have smoking or an executive suite." Mentwether turned to walk toward the elevator. Elaine called out good luck.

"Give us a suite. My woman deserves first class. Don't you deserve first class, honey?" The man slipped his arm around the woman's waist. She tucked her chin against his shoulder and laughed.

"Elaine, excuse me, would you mind assisting Mr…?"

"Call me Bill."

"Assisting Bill. And let me know if you hear any news."

"You have exactly ten minutes." Elaine's spiky hair stuck out on one side. The look she gave him would have turned up worms.

Room 170

Stan's fine dark hair smelled of fresh shampoo, his neck of soapy perspiration. Even though the weight of him made her arms ache, Monica clung to him like he was a supporting pillar. Ivan slung his arm around her waist, bumping her hip as they stumbled along, galloping like a four-legged animal with a suitcase toward their room by the exit. "Slow down," he said. "Take a deep breath. Monica, you're scaring me."

Still shaken by the strange occurrences in the room from which she had just escaped, Monica buried her face in Stan's sweet hair, stumbling up against Ivan until he said, "You haven't been drinking, have you?"

They made it back to Room 170. "Pack," she said, "we have to leave." There was nothing else to do; she needed to get far away quickly from the evil in that room, from the horribleness of the whole experience, call it their first ruined vacation, call it what Ivan wanted. She held onto to Stan and directed her ex-fiancé, "Go ahead, start packing."

He shook his head. He hadn't even bothered to buckle his belt after he received her call, just threw on his pants, picked Stan up, and started out to find her. "Monica, on the phone you screamed and said, 'Don't hurt me.' What the hell's going on?"

She said, "Don't curse," as Stan wiggled in her arms. He had to go to the potty.

She carried him to the bathroom. "Ivan, I want to go home. I don't like the Reds, I don't care about baseball." She put Stan down in front of the toilet. "You don't like swimming, I don't like baseball. What else do you want me to say?"

"Tell me what happened, or I'll call the front desk. Did some man try to attack you?"

"No," she shouted. There wasn't time. She didn't need the complications. Whatever was wrong with the room, it was best left alone. Maybe the sunlight would come in and kill it. If Ivan would just stop talking and pack, she might be able to gain necessary distance from the experience so she could sort it out from a delusional dream, baffling, troubling, what couldn't have happened.

But he wouldn't start packing, and the it remained, hovering and shimmering close enough to touch her. "If you're not going to pack, come help with Stan." She could gather their belongings better and faster, anyway. She didn't know if she'd be able to drive. She held out her hands. Her bare fingers trembled.

"Listen, Mon, you have to slow down." Ivan sat on the bed right in front of her and leaned forward, gesturing for Stan to come to him. "Tell me what happened, and then maybe we'll drive to Wooster in the middle of the night." He settled the boy into bed, tucked him under a sheet. "Night," the father said; "Night," the son. Ivan kissed Stan's forehead with his finger.

Their things were scattered everywhere, socks, a stray marble which Stan shouldn't play with because he sometimes absent-mindedly tucked things in his mouth, one of his shoelaces, but she didn't see the shoe. "Have you seen his shoe?"

"Monica, are you having some kind of breakdown?"

"The man who had the room before me. You should have seen it, it was a mess, drawers open, towels on the floor."

"How did you meet the man who had the room?"

Ivan, who'd been kicking around the floor, leaned over

and came up with Stan's shoe. Monica accepted it and shoved it in a backpack. "When I went, I just wanted to get a room, but they only had smoking or executive suites, so the clerk was looking for a cheaper room when this man, a tall man, came up and said he wanted another room, and I asked could I have his. It was already paid for, so it didn't cost anything. That's the man I mean."

"Why would you do that? What if he damaged something, or had another key?"

"He wasn't that kind of man. He looked normal, and he had a wife."

"If his wife wanted an executive suite, why didn't they get one in the first place?"

"I don't know, who knows? Stop asking questions. He said the room was haunted, but I said I didn't care about ghosts." She stripped Ivan's shirts from the hangers in the closet. "Something was wrong with the walls. There were echoes and things moved around, but it sounds crazy, I know it sounds crazy."

Ivan nodded as if he understood. In his dark eyes, TV lights danced. The volume was on mute, for which she was grateful. Suddenly her ears were very tired, sensitive to the point of tenderness, and even the electrical hum when the clock turned over a minute hurt to listen to. She scratched an itch on her inner left wrist.

"But I don't understand why you screamed."

"Because a phone book fell off the dresser."

"It was probably right on the edge."

"No, it wasn't, it was in the middle. I put it there myself. I don't want to talk about it, Ivan. It wasn't natural, it was something spooky. But that can't be true, I know it can't."

"Mon, whatever you say, I believe you. I was just asking a question."

"If you believe me, you'll get up and pack whatever's left."

"Okay," her ex-fiancé said, throwing up his hands. "I don't understand, but we'll head back to Wooster. You've been hard to understand all day. It's too late to give away the tickets to anybody."

"The baseball game won't miss us." She turned and said, "Ivan, thank you," throwing her arms around him because he was willing to go and soon she'd be far away, headed home, home, where phone books stayed in place. "Hurry up, I'll get Stan."

"Hey," Ivan said, rubbing his knuckles gently against the back of her neck. He smelled of the day's leftover aftershave, slightly gamy like standing in the wind.

"You're here and safe. I love you, and that's all that matters."

She wasn't ready for the future or love. "Don't forget the baby shampoo in the tub."

He sighed, dropping his arms. "Okay, give me a minute. If I'm going to drive all the way back to Ohio, I need some time to get ready." He went into the bathroom and shut the door.

Left alone in the Ivanless room, Monica sat on the bed and looked around. They were half packed up. Stan looked beautiful asleep, his skin perfectly smooth, like the fuzzy leaf of an elephant ear. In and out, the fall and rise of his chest, and he just kept breathing. If the night went on for a million minutes, the pattern wouldn't change. She was so tired. She lightly rubbed Stan's back. Her head drifted to the pillow. It wouldn't hurt to rest for a minute. She curled up next to the boy like a bean. She was glad now that Ivan had asked for a room on the end. They were about to experience an emergency exit. Cuddled beside Stan, she began not to believe, to give in to the buzzing in her head that blotted out wakefulness and flowed with scenery: an English garden, the moon's surface like a face, a dog running down a street.

When Ivan shook her shoulder, she bolted open her

eyes. She jumped and he jumped, apologizing and explaining, “I’m sorry, but if you want to go to Wooster, I had to wake you up.”

It felt too far to stand up. It felt too good to be sleeping. She was so tired, and Stan was tired too. The danger drifted further away. Did he mind if she slept for a while?

“How long is a while?”

Probably until morning. She’d wake up early. That was what she always did.

Something, “change your mind again.” Silence. He kissed her cheek and said, “Tomorrow, we have to talk.”

That was all she wanted in the first place. To go to sleep, to travel toward tomorrow. She still didn’t want to go to St. Louis, but in the morning they’d figure it out: everything could wait, nothing couldn’t wait.

“One more thing,” he said, “what about the ring?”

“What about the ring?” she asked from inside her dreams, feeling him slip it on her finger. It was looser than before, it spun around. She shook her hand and it flew off. “What happened to the tape?”

“I cut it off. I thought I’d be taking it back.”

She didn’t know, but it was too big for her finger without tape. If she wore it, she’d lose it in the sheets.

"Not tonight. Put it somewhere safe. Put it in your pocket."

"Does that mean you still want to get married?"

But it was too late. A wave of exhaustion overcame her.

Ivan was left holding the ring. He decided to store it in his wallet. If he put it in his pocket, it might fall out. He slid it next to the cash he carried to buy them all souvenirs and food at Busch Stadium, where they probably would never arrive if Monica didn't change her mind. The important thing was, she was back in the room which had to mean something. He pulled off his clothes for the second time and dropped them on the floor, crawling into the opposite bed. On the one hand, he didn't want to be the man that could lose a woman like her. On the other hand, if she didn't want him, he should let go like a hot wire. The thing was, he was certain, absolutely certain, that he could love her like she wanted to be loved, that if they stuck together, time would work out the kinks. Ivan knew he had staying power. She was worth the effort; he loved her and both of them could change.

In the morning, that's what he'd tell her. It was true,

she was a morning person. Ivan shut off the light and settled into bed, increasing the volume of the TV slightly, just loud enough that he could hear. He liked to sleep with TV in the background. He didn't know how Monica would feel about the fact. He'd deal with it when he had to.

⁂ Room 233 ⁂

The party was over before it started. There weren't too many supplies. If they split the vodka, it would have been a swallow each. Gus said the girl should drink it all since she was starting late. Her highlighted hair was long and straight, as sleek as a hot iron could make it. She barely sipped the first time, coughed and made a face, looked too cute when she puckered her lips. Gus said, "Like this," and motioned bottoms up.

Allisandra lit a cigarette. The girl, whose name she'd already forgotten, took the shot like Gus told her, slamming it and shivering her shoulders. Jessie fired up what was left of the blunt. Gus instructed the girl how to hit. She said, "I've smoked a couple of times. I'm not a complete baby."

She claimed she was seventeen, a junior, but Allisandra didn't believe it. Her presence was an annoying development. It must have been the vodka. The Gus she'd known since he first came to Belzer didn't pick up random infants. He only went with girls from other schools who never hung around long. As far as she knew, he'd never had a real girlfriend. Tonight she wanted him all by himself, but then he brought the girl back.

The girl inhaled and held the smoke, leaning forward to pass to Allisandra, who said, "I don't want it. Give it to him." She nudged Jessie with her elbow. With his spine relaxed and his hands between his knees, her boyfriend reminded her of an ape, dazed out on TV after getting his rocks off. She didn't love him, but she liked how he wanted her, how he lost control of his words: *Baby, yeah, you uh my oh, are you ready*, draw back her hips, *no, uh come back, do you*, arch her back, *stop it, I'm going to uh*. Sex with Jesse wasn't like when she touched herself, not as vivid, more muted like static, like riding a rocking horse to nowhere and not caring when she didn't get there.

Gus took the girl's hand and put it on his leg. She slapped his jeans and pulled her hand away. "I have a boyfriend in St. Louis, but we're probably breaking up because of my mother."

"Where is she?" Allisandra asked.

The girl giggled. Gus found her hand again. She laughed, reaching for the blunt. "Sleeping. She likes her Ambien."

Jessie confiscated the roach and tamped it out, storing it in a cellophane. "Ambien's good for a party. Why don't you snag us a couple?"

"I could, but my aunt, she's a bitch. Her or one of my cousins would wake up. No way could I could get in and out of the room."

"That blows, man. I could crush on some Ambien. Makes everything go wavy."

Gus leaned from his seat on the box springs, pulled the girl's chair around to face him, then slipped his arm around the girl's waist. "Hey," she said, "stop it, that tickles." She looked to Allisandra. "Can you believe Mr. Hands?"

The girl was absolutely not right for Gus. "Where does your aunt think you are?"

"If he's Mr. Hands, can I be Mr. Boobs?" her boyfriend put in, reaching for her chest.

"Cut it out. You had yours already. Finish your smoke and let's go."

"Come on," Gus said. "It's early. Cara hasn't even

kissed me." He looked up at the girl, pouting with his bottom lip.

She kissed her finger with a loud smack and pressed it against his mouth. "There you go. I need to use the bathroom. This way, right?" She stood up, wobbling once, laughing, went in and shut the door, skinny and leggy in pink gym shorts.

In spite of the open window, smoke hung in the dimly lit room. The Discovery channel was still on, something about the extinction of hippos. Allisandra dropped ashes into a plastic cup, raising a hiss from the water.

Gus fell back on the box springs. On his back, he stared hard at the ceiling. He looked less substantial lying on the bed, slighter inside his rumpled clothes. He was taller than Allisandra but shorter than Jessie. She had hugged him once at a funeral and was surprised by his wiry strength, muscles strung thick along solid bones. He had a reputation for being a badass, but she'd never seen him in a fight. He said, "I need to sit up." His voice sounded thick as syrup. He was still lying there when Cara came from the bathroom. He patted a spot on the bed. "I've been saving this seat for you."

Any intelligent girl would have laughed in his face, but Cara didn't have any brains. She reminded Allisandra of the middle school girls who waited for the bus at the corner across from the old gas station, little sluts who shouted at passing cars, "Give us a ride," or, "Hey, man, you're hot." Little prick teases wouldn't know what to do if a car actually pulled over.

Cara sat down and asked, "Where do you want me?"

Gus pulled himself halfway up. He looked like hell, his eyes dull and bloodshot, a faint mustache above his upper lip, but when he smiled at the girl, Allisandra wanted to slap her. She dropped her cigarette in the cup and placed it on the nightstand, leaning across Jessie who ran a hand down her back and slid it into her jeans.

"Watch it," she said, "we have company."

"It didn't bother you an hour ago."

"That was then and this is now. It's time for me to go home."

"Go on then." Gus was leaning back, his arm behind the girl, who rested against him watching TV, a commercial about Alaskan cruises.

"Have you ever been on a cruise?" she asked. "I'm afraid I'd get seasick."

"Shit, I heard everything's included, the booze, all you can eat. Steak, shrimp, even lobster, man."

"I know what we can do," the girl said. "Let's sneak

into the pool. I feel like going swimming."

It was too late to go swimming, two strikes against the idea; too late and there'd be double trouble because they weren't legally registered. "No one's swimming," Allisandra insisted. "It's too late. The party's over."

"I told you, go on home then." Gus scowled at her from the box springs like she was trying to ruin his fun.

It wasn't her fault it was getting late. "Don't you have to work tomorrow?"

"Hey," Jessie said, "what do you care? You think you're his mother or something?"

What had started out as a hotel party night was turning out lame. "Fine, you stay, too, then. I can get home on my own." Allisandra stood up and shouldered her purse.

"You're leaving?" The girl looked up from the bed, for the first time appearing concerned.

"Yeah, you stay and have all the fun you want with Mr. Hands and Mr. Boobs."

"Hey," Jessie said, "don't start that shit."

"I'm not starting shit, I'm ending shit."

Jessie gave up. "I guess I have to go, too, man." He stood, shoved one hand in his hip pocket, brushed back his lank hair with the other.

Cara said, "I guess I'll go, too."

"No," Gus said. "Stay and party. We'll have the whole room to ourselves."

She giggled. "You wish. If my aunt wakes up, she'll send out a party, a search party."

"You're kidding, right? I thought you said she was sleeping."

The girl shrugged. "I told you, she's a bitch."

"Let's get out of here." Allisandra looked around the room. They hadn't done that much damage, only removed a few souvenirs, the little bottles of shampoo and lotion, an ink pen embossed Meridian Inn.

The girl stood up. "It was fun. You ought to give me your e-mail."

"I don't have one," Gus said. He didn't move. "I used to have a cell phone."

"Come on." Allisandra didn't want to abandon him. It felt right that they should all leave together, just as they'd arrived, minus the girl who was headed toward the door. Good riddance to the little slut.

Jessie yawned. "Come on, Ally. Leave the man alone." Gus was lying on the box springs on his back again, staring at the ceiling.

She didn't want to leave him there, but she followed Jessie out. In the parking lot, the girl looked and waved.

Allisandra and Jessie turned the other way, headed toward the sidewalk. The night was darker, deeper than before, no moon in the hazy sky. In spite of the traffic, their steps sounded loud on the dry grass and then the pavement. “I don’t think we should have left Gus. What if he falls asleep? They might call it trespassing.”

“Don’t worry, he’s a big boy. You act like you like him or something.”

She told Jessie not to be stupid. She said, “If I wanted Gus, I could have him.” It wasn’t true, but until she said it out loud, she didn’t want to admit it. It was one of those truths like a slammed door. When they passed the street light where insects swarmed, a moth landed and caught in her hair. She jumped and danced, trying to knock it out, while Jessie laughed and said, “Hold still.” Afterwards, she wouldn’t hold his hand. She said, “It’s too hot. I don’t want to be touched. I’d rather walk alone.”

Room 205

When Merry shook Genevieve's shoulder, her sister levitated. Her sleeping form rose up from the mattress, arm swinging as she shouted, "What?" Her eyes opened, glaringly alert, before they dropped and she fell back to sleep. Merry stepped back, stumbled, sat down hard on the opposite bed. The glow of the TV hardened her resolve. "Genevieve," she whispered, dropping to her knees between the beds and sticking her face close to her sister's. "Genevieve, wake up. Cara's missing from the van."

Her sister's eyes once more shot open, radiating indignation. "What? What?" she shouted, snorting and blinking before settling back unaware.

Up close, Genevieve's lower lip trembled and her eyes sank beneath the lids. Merry didn't know much about sleeping pills, but her sister must have taken a strong one.

She sat on the floor, leaned back against the bed where Julie slightly stirred. All the times Merry had rescued Genevieve: cleaning up after parties when their parents left town, unlocking the windows so she could sneak in, listening to her for weeks and hours on the phone whenever her marriages went bad. Maybe it wasn't exactly shocking news that Genevieve needed strong sleeping pills. But to be put to sleep to the point that she couldn't be waked even in the event of an emergency: what if there was a fire? Someone else would be responsible for dragging her unconscious body from the building.

Their father always said Genevieve was a born insomniac, but their mother said that wasn't it. Their mother said some babies were born with their days and nights mixed up, and that not prayer or parents could fix it. Their mother did everything to keep Genevieve awake during the day when she was a baby, rubbing ice cubes across her feet, poking her with a fingernail, holding her up in front of the freezing exhaust of a window unit air conditioner. Nothing ever opened her baby blue eyes except the sun going down. If it had ended then, but Genevieve was a night-awake toddler, a grade schooler dozing in her cereal, a high school cheerleader always late to morning practice, a college girl who slept through her classes until she decided to drop out and get married. For her wedding gift the first time around, she asked Merry for a coffee pot with a timer. The second time, she bought one herself. She never wanted to be responsible for waking up early to make a man's morning beverage.

There were a hundred family stories about Genevieve, but only one that featured Merry as a baby. When she was six months old, she almost ate a caterpillar that fell out of a tree onto her baby blanket. The girls got hysterical every time their grandmother told it. It wasn't the worst story to have. In her solitary bed, Genevieve shuddered in her sleep. One o'clock was approaching.

Merry turned and rested her head on the mattress. She needed to stay awake until Cara was found, but it wouldn't hurt to close her eyes for a minute. If it were Jessica or Janet, or God forbid, Julie, she'd have already called the police. Of course, she would never have allowed her daughters to sleep in a van in the parking lot in the first place. Their parents had raised them better. At fifteen and sixteen, Merry and Genevieve still lived under an iron curtain curfew. Not that it had kept either one of them out of trouble in the long run, but it had held trouble at bay for a while. She had only herself to blame for her later mistakes, the pregnancy and ending it. Why did she have to think of it when the Bible said, *Ask and ye shall be forgiven*? The surfacing of the memory always flushed her with shame. *Dear God*, she prayed, *please don't let the girls find out. Don't let them repeat my mistake.*

Sitting slumped against the side of the bed, Merry's lower back complained. She forced her tired eyes open. If she fell asleep and Cara was still missing in the morning, she'd never forgive herself. Someone had to be responsible. An executive decision needed to be made. Now that Genevieve and Cara were living back in Pitt, things were going to change. Merry took a deep breath and closed her eyes, praying for strength and guidance. There was no choice but to inform the authorities, though she didn't want to wake the girls. She'd go back to the front desk for assistance. The manager guy was no help—men!—but at least Elaine showed concern.

Front Lobby

I.

Duncan left Elaine at the front desk and went into the manager's office, ostensibly to finish his sandwich. First, however, he decided to call Housekeeping to check on Room 212. Floretta answered and said, "I'll go check on that room after towel inventory is finished." She wasn't so old, maybe mid-forties, but her hair was completely white, long past her shoulders, wavy and stringy, clipped back on top with a spotty metal barrette. She was short, and when she walked, she leaned forward, which caused her feet to turn out. Or maybe the splayed feet came first, which caused the forward leaning. Duncan could never decide.

He said, "Sounds good. Give me a call back. Let me know how you find things." If he had time, he'd go check the room himself, but at the moment, he had other worries. Once he was off the phone, he surveyed his leftover sandwich and touched the cover of Volume 8 mindlessly, his fingers massaging its texture. The missing girl mystery multiplied with meaning in the gray brightness of the insular office. The little wenchlet was probably playing hooky, escaping from something larger than Room 205, from the stifling confines of a minivan childhood and all the demands and restrictions that came with it. But there was still the possibility of foul play, however unlikely the odds. If the girl had managed to get herself abducted by a serial killer, or even a one time sociopathic opportunist, it could come back to bite him in the ass. The aunt, Mentwether, had seemed plenty worked up. He envisioned if worse came to worse: lawsuits, negative publicity, the embarrassment of a trial. The question: Why did you wait a second to report the girl missing to the police?

The least he could do would be to give Marian a heads up, make a small preemptive strike. He had called her at home before with verifiable emergencies, incidents accompanied by ambulances and/or EMT personnel, not to mention law enforcement.

By this time of night, she'd be tucked into bed, wearing sensible pajamas or one of those sleeveless nightgowns made of nylon with the little bow between the breasts, something practical and feminine, not a sloppy t-shirt or sexy fuck-me teddy, though if she ever wanted to wear a fuck-me teddy, especially red, he was certain she'd look spectacular.

She answered on the first ring. "Yes?" She didn't even say hello.

"Hey, Marian, this is Duncan. We have a little problem here." He waited to see what she wanted to know, but the phone remained silent. "Marian?"

"I'm here. What is it? Just tell me. I haven't been to sleep."

Insomnia? The personal business she'd mentioned? Possibly she'd been out with a stalker idiot, some jerk still skulking around her apartment like he owned the place. "A guest stopped by the desk and said her niece is missing. I don't think it's an emergency yet, but I thought I should give you a heads up."

"When did this happen?"

"Twenty minutes ago. She last saw the girl at ten."

Had he checked with Housekeeping and Maintenance? Yes, they'd been notified. "She's only been missing a couple of hours. She probably just wandered off."

"How old is she? What's her name?"

"Fifteen, sixteen. Her aunt called her Cara."

"I really don't need this tonight."

He tried to lighten the mood. "I don't we think we need to make a federal case out of it yet. You know how kids are today. Another hour or two, I'll bet she shows up."

Marian didn't take the bait. "Have you started an incident report?"

No, but he would, now that she mentioned it.

"I guess I'll have to come in."

The last time she arrived in the middle of the night, gale-force winds had caused a power outage. Even though electricity was restored in an hour, she stayed until the system rebooted. It was one of Duncan's top five memories, along with catching a foul ball in the stands at the old stadium before they built Victory Field, and the winter he was the Scottish High Priest of beer bottle bowling in college while wearing his clan's kilt.

He and Marian had kicked back behind the front desk, and she told him about her childhood. When she was a little kid, she'd thought they named the county after her, but she'd thought they made a spelling mistake, that Marion County should be spelled Marian.

She said, "I'm on my way. If the girl shows up, give

me a call on my cell." Her voice grew fainter like she'd turned her head. "No, you're going with me."

"Where am I going?" Duncan wanted to know.

"Not you, it's my brother. I'll be there as soon as I can."

Duncan hung up the phone. A brother. He hadn't known she had one. He went to the filing cabinets to retrieve an incident report. Not that brothers were inherently problematic, but certainly a complication. Older or younger? Birth order made a difference. Older, and there could be protectiveness issues, the Knight Valiant on his raging steed, challenging all comers like they were after his sister with raging, flaming hard-ons.

Younger brothers, in Duncan's opinion, usually had fewer issues. He was a younger brother, and though his oldest sister Karoline frequently called him irresponsible, he usually showed up sober on holidays, and had helped move her furniture, and Miranda's, too, more than once in his life, back-breaking boxes and couches, for nothing more than goodwill and beer. In addition, he always remembered their birthdays, which were luckily two days apart.

With the incident report in hand, he walked out to the lobby. At the lower front desk, Elaine was on the phone.

He rapped his knuckles on the counter. “Hey, hang up and you’re out of here. You can log off whenever you want.” Who needed her when Marian was coming in?

The assistant clerk shot him a baleful look. She swiveled back and forth in her chair, monitoring the movie audit. She removed the phone from the crook of her neck and deliberately replaced the receiver. “She’s not answering. Thanks for nothing.”

“Look, it’s not my fault Ryan’s a clumsy guy.”

“It’s not about fault, it’s about my life. I should have been home an hour ago.”

“If lover girl calls, I’ll say you’re on your way.”

“Don’t do me any favors.” When Elaine was unhappy, her lips contracted into a small, wrinkled line that did nothing to improve her appearance. Duncan decided against mentioning the phenomenon. He turned to the counter to begin the report. It was a multi-functional document used to record information that didn’t necessarily require mechanical or housekeeping maintenance, more of an opinion form for strongly worded complaints or to capture eye-witness evidence, with relevant sections for explanations: How did the situation come to your attention? What happened next? And next?

He could hear Elaine shutting down the computer, slamming a drawer, rattling her car keys. "Have a good weekend," he said without looking when she brushed behind him to leave.

"Sure, you, too," she responded disconsolately, but at least she'd managed the right words. He knew, in a pinch, she could pull it together. She had the bounce-back power of a rubber ball.

Absent-mindedly, he updated his log-in. The lobby lights made small tight shadows around the edges of the fake potted plants. Nothing was stirring, not a guest, not a car. On the other side of the couches, beyond the glass-paneled wall, the swimming pool continued to glow blue, an iridescent aqua like Neptune, whose color was attributed to an as-yet-unidentified chromophore that gave the gaseous planet its tint. If it hadn't been for his congenital mathematical disability, Duncan would have picked science over history. In the end, parabolas did him in. He could never make them shift quadrants.

In the predawn quiet, he worked on the incident report, filling in blanks as thoroughly as possible. When the elevator dinged, he looked up. Mentwether turned the corner. She was traveling alone and didn't look happy. He called, "Have any luck?"

Mentwether shook her head, approaching with effort, her cheeks flushed with agitation. “Where’s Elaine?”

He, too, wished Elaine could take care of things, but it looked like the two of them were stuck. “She’s gone for the night. What can I do for you?”

The woman gave an audible sigh. It seemed that her sister had taken a sleeping pill. Merry couldn’t wake her up. “I’ve made up my mind. It’s time to contact the authorities. I want to call the police and report that my niece, Cara Ann Baker, is missing.”

“Okay, we can do that.” But he wanted to finish the incident report first. It was only one o’clock.

“You hear it every day on the news, how girls get molested and murdered. What about the little girl in Florida? What about Samantha Runnion? I don’t even want to think about it, the very idea makes me sick.” Her body shuddered with visceral empathy.

The feeling was almost transferable, but he resisted because even the most vivid imagining wouldn’t make the girl appear. “Before we make the call, I’d still like to finish the report. Do you mind if I ask you a few questions?”

Mentwether had a solid version of events, beginning with Cara’s overall bad attitude, leading to her unreasonable parking lot demand, how Merry made sure she was safe by watching through the window next to the ice machine, how she went back to the room and dozed off, waking up with a bad dream. "And what happened then?" Duncan asked, pen poised to write it down.

"I went out to the van to check on her and she was gone."

"Have you checked the van again?"

Mentwether shook her head. "I took the keys and locked it up. Isn't that report finished?"

Duncan was once again agreeing that law enforcement was the next logical step when Marian's car pulled into the entry bay. She got out, not in her navy blazer but wearing a sweatshirt and jeans. Her hair, pulled back in a ponytail, made her look ten years younger. She stopped and leaned over, speaking to someone reclined in the passenger seat.

He had thought she would bring her brother inside, but maybe this way was better. He said, "That's our office manager, Marian Carravejo. I called her for assistance." Would he have noticed her back in high school? On the one hand, probably not. His tastes back then were flashier, blonder.

"Marian," he said when she walked in, "this is Mrs.

Mentwether, whose niece is missing. She thinks we should call the police."

Mentwether responded by apologizing, "I shouldn't be the one who's bothering you tonight. My girls are sound asleep. But Cara's mother, my sister Genevieve, took a sleeping pill and I can't wake her up."

A door opened and shut down a hallway. A buzzing approached from the back. Floretta wandered into the lobby leaning on a wide cordless broom. "Any news on the girl?" she said over its motor. "I'm going to check 212 now."

"What's wrong with 212?" Marian put her hands on her hips.

Duncan winked at her to let her know the problem was negligible. He'd fill in the details later. "Nothing much. Thanks, Floretta." He waved so she would keep moving.

Mentwether asked, "Should you call or should I? I didn't want to do it from the room because I didn't want to wake up my girls."

Marian looked over the incident report while the two of them waited. "Okay," she said finally. "Duncan can call the police in the office. I'll wait here with Merry; may I call you Merry?"

"Yes," the woman said, "like Christmas."

Marian turned and her eyes lit on Duncan. "Don't you have a call to make?"

Up close, she didn't look younger. Dark circles smiled above her cheek bones, and her lips were dry, flaky. If he had lip balm, he would have offered her some. Maybe she was tired, but Elaine had had a point; something was up with Marian.

In the office, a peculiar, sour odor greeted him. The pastrami in his sandwich, now unrefrigerated for too many hours, had curled and ripened on his desk, which was cluttered not only with his thermos and Volume 8 of the *Merits Students Encyclopedia*, but also with the afternoon receipts and the turned-down photographs that belonged to Henry, the guy who shared the desk.

Duncan turned up the photographs, arranging them as the other night supervisor kept them, in a shrine-like semi-circle. The pictures were of the slob's new baby, a kid so fat, she looked like bowling ball. It wasn't that she was ugly, but the pictures demanded attention, a googly-eyed fat baby whose eyes followed you everywhere like a dummy portrait in a B-horror movie. Duncan wrapped up the leftover sandwich in a baggie and shoved it into the brown paper sack, sealing it tight to contain the smell before tossing it in the trash. He fanned Volume 8 around to freshen the air, then slipped it into his backpack. He wasn't actually stealing the book; he only wanted to borrow it. If the previous owner ever showed up, he or she could have it back *tout suite.*

He stood up, stretching, and the thermos of coffee he'd finished earlier reminded him he had a bladder. The police could wait a few more minutes. He went into the private office facilities. He'd already decided to call the main line instead of 911. The missing girl was the possibility of an emergency, not yet an actual event, though the dispatcher would send a squad car over. Maybe they'd get lucky and get decent cops. A few of them existed, even cops with a sense of humor, or more than two grains of intelligence, like that guy, the brother of someone's sister, who saved a woman's life because he could tell something wasn't right, and sure enough, the ex-boyfriend had a gun. On the other hand were the lugheads who abused their civil authority like it was a second dick and they had four hands. He wasn't opposed to cops at the level of civil order; he liked walking in safety down the street as much as anyone, but then he'd never been manhandled, beaten, or arrested for some non-offense like the color of his skin, driving in the wrong neighborhood, or being drunk and belligerent in public. Okay, he'd been drunk and belligerent in public, but that got him gut-punched, not arrested. It hadn't been a cop who gut-punched him, either, just some asshole who stepped out of an alley.

He zipped up, hating the gut-puncher and the memory of the pain, washed his hands and went out to his desk.

A distinct screaming penetrated the office. He knew right away it was Marian. He leaped up and in four large steps reached the door, flung it open, and stepped out behind the desk. Marian, in motion, met his acceleration, not a gut punch but a definite thwack that sent him reeling back so his head banged the door jamb, an impact so sharp that he saw stars and had to blink one eye.

Marian didn't keep her feet. She got knocked back and landed on the floor. Mentwether stared and he noticed the girl, Cara, who had returned from prodigal to the fold. It was the same jailbait he'd seen earlier walking down the stairs. She didn't seem any worse for the wear, wide-eyed and emanating hostility. He wondered where she'd come from, where she had been. He leaned over, rubbed the back of his head and offered Marian his hand. "What's going on? Where'd she come from? Let me help you up."

"No," she said, waving him away, hiding her face between her knees. "Not yet. Wait a minute." Her shoulders heaved and then went still, though her body still trembled with breathing.

He looked from his boss to the speechless guests. "Hello, Merry. What's going on?"

"The boy in the car," Mentwether answered, "I think the young man stole her car. It started and he drove off."

"Not stolen," Marian muffled without raising her head. "Borrowed, not stolen."

Her brother and the car were definitely missing from the entry bay. "Is your brother coming back?"

Cara, whose interest had dwindled to a preoccupation with the terra cotta floor, looked up with visible disdain. "Who cares? Can we go to our room? If I have to sleep in this stupid hotel, I don't want to stand all night in the lobby."

Mentwether yawned. "Now you're worried about sleeping. If it hadn't been for you, everyone would be asleep."

"Wait," Marian said, pushing up from the floor before Duncan could reach again to help her. She dusted off her jeans and smoothed her sweatshirt. Duncan rubbed his head. He wasn't seeing stars any more, but the lobby still moved; as he watched, it wobbled on its axis.

She said, “You need to sign the incident report. Duncan can finish it up.”

“Where are you going? Are you leaving all ready? How are you getting home?” The last thing he knew, they were calling the police. The knock on his head was tender, bruised, a painful lump. It was better to swell out than to swell in in order to avoid concussion; he knew that from general reading. What he needed was ice. He said, “Excuse me,” and reached around Marian to get a cold pack from the first aid station beneath the counter.

Marian’s voice cut into his dizziness: “Look, either you can finish the report or I can, and it’s not going to be me.”

He pressed the cold pack to the lump on his head. She didn’t even notice he was wounded. “Okay, sure, whatever you say.”

She thanked Mentwether for her time and patience. “If you’ll just sign the report before you go, we need it for our records.” She turned and went into the manager’s office without a backwards glance.

II.

Marian entered the office. The closed blinds

stared at her blankly. Collapsing into the chair at the nearest desk, the one nobody ever used because the drawers were locked and the key had been lost, she rolled forward and sunk her head in her arms on its cool, gray surface. She had left her keys in the car so Jared could listen to his music. The never-ending saga of life loosened like bands that would twist and stretch if she had to confront another turn. She took deep breaths and concentrated on feeling the pressure of her forehead against her arm, the warm fuzzy feeling of skin turned pillow. In the cave of trapped breath, the scents of fabric softener and deodorant swirled with her body, sweet mixed with stress.

It happened so fast, the girl appearing in the entrance doors. Jared sat up in the car to walk her watch in, and then Merry was shouting, "Thank God, you're all right." Marian only wanted to excuse herself, to tell Duncan they didn't need the police. Merry said, "Is that smoke? Do I smell smoke?" and Cara blamed a bonfire on the beach, but there wasn't a beach. She was lying, clearly lying. Merry accused her of being nothing but trouble. This nice lady had to come to work, and everyone was upset; what kind of example was she setting for the girls, when a sound so small that it was like a rain drop falling into the bucket of Merry's harangue caused Marian to turn her head. Her brother was behind the wheel of the car she was so proud of. When she bought it, the silver Saturn SL was pristine clean and had only fifty-thousand miles. When he started the engine, she didn't understand. And then the headlights flashed on. What was he doing? She knew what he was doing, but he was still doing it anyway.

In the tiny little cave, she tightened her shoulders in order to release them and roll away the tension. She had to roll them three times. She hated it that she had screamed. What, did she think she could stop Jared? She had bribed him, forced him, to come with her in the first place. She couldn't have left him at their grandmother's place; his coming and going was killing the woman. Jared's lifestyle would snap anybody's nerves, and their grandmother was too old to deal with it. She complained the phone rang all the time, different numbers, and unidentifiable voices. She said all the ringing would run up the bill, when what she meant was it made her anxious, an old woman that needed her peace. What was Jared thinking? She hated him, hated him, for taking advantage of their grandmother, of her, for driving off in her car.

She would never have let him drive her car. His

license was suspended. It wasn't the car, she would see it again, but him, who cared so little, no respect for anyone, anything, their grandmother, their mother, himself. Running loose and in trouble because, but she could only imagine because she was not him, something gone wrong, a stream of something wrongs, yes, his father, not their uncle, just because of one, the other, but not always so. He was someone else. Her brother could be someone else if he wanted.

Duncan knocked on the door before coming in. Marian raised her head, rolled her neck, blinked open and rubbed her eyes. She couldn't sleep here. Maybe he was back. She yawned and looked at Duncan. "Did my brother come back?"

He pulled a cold pack away from the back of his head. He must have bumped it when they collided. She asked, "Are you okay?"

"Nothing two aspirin won't take care of. What about you?" He turned the pack over in his meaty hands and reapplied it. "Look, I don't mean to get personal, but something's going on." He sat down at his desk across the office. "It's been a crazy night."

Morning. It was already morning. He was only three inches taller than Marian, but when he leaned back in his desk chair with legs extended, and his arm crooked behind his head to keep the cold pack in place, he looked like he could've been seven feet tall. She apologized. "Somebody had to finish the report."

"I know, and it had to be me." He swung around and touched the keyboard to activate his computer screen. "So, she just walked in. I had a feeling. You know these crazy kids. What's up with your brother and the car?"

If she knew what was up with her brother and the car, she wouldn't be sitting here. "He'll bring it back, I just don't know when." She thought of her mother, and how her protection served like a mark on the wall to measure height, to measure growth. How could Marian and her brother have been raised by the same woman?

"All I want to know is, did you know your brother was taking the car? Otherwise, technically, it's theft." Duncan put down the cold pack and keyed up the reconciliation report, striking the Enter key to initiate the program.

"Don't worry about him. He's my problem."

Duncan mumbled something, but she didn't ask him to repeat it. It was too late to call anyone, she'd have to take a cab, though she didn't have enough cash. She'd already bought Jared cigarettes, not to mention tacos for dinner.

"Can I borrow ten dollars?"

"Sure," Duncan said, scooting back, and taking out his wallet. She didn't mention that he'd loosened his tie. He didn't ask why she needed money. He said, "I just want you to know, I never thought the girl was in trouble. You never had to come in."

It was her job to respond to emergencies. She didn't owe him an explanation. "Thanks for the loan. I'll pay you back." She tried to open the top drawer to find a phone book, then remembered the desk was permanently locked. There was a phone book in the lobby where she could also watch for a cab. "I'll wait at the front desk. I'll let you know when I'm going."

"Sure, okay," he said, turning his back. "Why don't you do that?"

His navy blazer stretched tight across his shoulders. She felt she had been abrupt. "Hey, don't worry, it'll all be okay. It's already tomorrow."

"Yeah," he said, "tomorrow's here. Let's have a celebration."

He had always struck her as a good coworker, competent, if on the dry side. The bad attitude was brand new. "Maybe you should celebrate on the weekend. You're off the schedule, right?"

"Yeah, off the schedule, that describes it." He waved good-bye over his shoulder. "Take care. See you later."

In the lobby, Marian leaned against the front desk and waited for her taxi. She was so tired, her thoughts came in waves that overlapped and wiped each other out. She was done with her brother. She was crazy worried about her brother. She would not forgive him for this. She would have to forgive him; she could not not forgive him. Once she got her car back, she'd never speak to him again.

When the taxi pulled in, she knocked twice on the office door. "I'm leaving," she called and went out. She looked up and down the parking lot and the four lanes of street. If her brother drove up right now, she knew she'd forgive him. But he didn't, and she despised the impulse. She got into the taxi and gave her address. She leaned back and closed her eyes. Wherever Jared was, he lived and flashed like the moving beams that flashed across her face. She could feel them, sense them, and the sensation was real. Her brother was gone. He was lost to her.

Another Day

The angels arrived at long last to rendezvous with Dorissa and Don. There were two of them, Harjo and Leminisse, assigned to the Millards' recovery and transport. It wasn't their job to evaluate the quality of the dead, whatever forms the remains assumed, only to locate and guide the aftereffects of life to the destination in their orders, in this case a central holding station that resembled loosely the concept of a forest, which surveys showed was universally accepted across a range of beliefs as a site where waiting would be the least disagreeable.

As angels went, Harjo and Leminisse looked the part—white-robed, bewinged, moving invisible beyond understanding, not professing legs or torsos, their integrity as identities achieved through transcendent means, not the least of which was a shared predilection for earthly rain, for the various textures of suspended water, from deep humidity to slashing droplets, because, they agreed, it tickled. Something about the vibration, they guessed, of moisture and the immaterial.

It wasn't their intent to go on an extended rain-chasing excursion, but in the meantime, what was the hurry? Once dead, the dead remained. If along the way, hurricanes or inland storms attracted them, the angels gave in to temptation. Eventually, they agreed, they would locate the Millards by a circuitous route, guided by shifting patterns of water and air. Whenever the angels became saturated, they couldn't help laughing out loud. It was like being at the mercy of a feather duster wielded by a benevolent power while they enacted the pretense of getting away. Some angels chased after the merciless sun; only a few preferred the bitterness of snow. One angel they knew had a thing for the smell of leather. Harjo said, "To each angel's own."

Leminisse agreed. They were both so agreeable. Never once had they argued. They left that for the dead, who were certainly no angels, but often quite disturbed, insisting that their lives had been cut short, that death so far hadn't been fair, that they wanted another shot at remorse, revenge, fortune or fame, great passion or greater folly. The angels paid no attention to complaints or desires. "Come along, please," they said in unison, as if the dead had a choice. The authority of angels was absolute in that they had the power to force the dead to move, though sometimes, if the remains were particularly agreeable, Harjo would suggest that the dead might like to lead, to which Leminisse replied, "A wonderful idea." With the dead in charge of the so-called reins, the angels rode along behind, their wing tips fluttering, not as exciting as rain, but not the worst way to travel the afterworld.

They always hoped for the best. They were idealistic angels. It was what they talked about during their rain-chasing, struck by drops of fat green water from a rain forest canopy, buffeted by tsunami-force horizontal streams, taking a soak as deep as a sauna in a rice field near a river.

"Isn't it nice when the dead greet us nicely?"

"I agree, that's always nice."

"I love it when the remains announce who they are."

"Oh, yes, I like to know names."

"I hate to admit it, but I'm bad with names. I never seem to remember who the dead are."

"Oh, me, too, I'm horrible with names. Please, don't feel bad."

"What do you think when the dead don't say anything?"

"That, I don't really mind."

"Me, either, not when they come along nicely."

"Oh, I absolutely agree."

They were conversing thus in coastal Karnataka during the Southwest Monsoon when a crash of thunder vibrated between them. It had only happened once before, a retrieval in the indefinite past. Close thunder was not a welcome sign. It could only mean one thing.

"Maybe we should move along, though isn't the rain nice?"

"Very nice, a good soaking rain."

"Do you think we should go around or over?"

"Which way is the wind blowing?"

"Oh, it's blowing either way."

"Then I'd say over."

"Yes, I agree. Should we leave right away?"

"I think we should. What do you think?"

"I say yes. Good-bye, sweet rain."

"Adios, adieu."

Over they went, slowing only to gaze at the black slate water of the Arctic, quiet and dark as granite next to ice mountains like crystals, melting, all melting away. "That beauty doth undo me," said Harjo.

Leminisse responded, "Please, wax poetic."

"I am undone as beauty doth do unto dark gray water in clouds that doth billow on yonder horizon."

It was true, a storm was brewing, but the angels had no more time. "I don't trust myself to go through it. Shall we go over or around?"

"Oh, over it. What do you think?"

"Over it sounds fine," and so up and over the storm they went, up and over the globe, to recover the Millards, who only the afternoon before had finally reached the Meridian Inn.

It was not the ideal situation. These were not ideal remains. Harjo said, "Oh, dear. Which one do you want?"

"I don't know, what about you?"

"It's difficult to know. The little one. Hello, excuse me, what was your name?" It was protocol to ask for verification reasons, and also out of general politeness. If the dead said nothing, that was excellent, as long as they moved along when instructed.

The papery one in a uniform saluted and shouted something unintelligible.

But the little one, a flickery light, said, *If you're from heaven, you should know my name. How do I know you're real angels?*

The papery one shouted and pointed his flat arm while kicking at a chair.

"Oh, dear," said Leminisse. "Combative behavior. Look, what we know is that you're destined for a predetermined and temporary location."

"Yes, a nice place. It resembles a forest."

What makes you think I care about a forest? I left Oklahoma to get away from the woods. I like cities; I want a city. I want to stay in a hotel.

"Maybe you'll get to, who knows?" said Harjo. "I think I'll take the paper remains."

"Oh, dear," said Leminisse. "That's what I was thinking."

Why don't you both take him? I can just stay here.

"But we can't . . ." the angels started together, "you must be recovered, transported, and delivered to the proper destination."

"What must be, must be," Harjo added kindly. "Que sera, sera."

"We can do this hard way or the easy way," Leminisse said to Harjo. "You choose, I don't care."

"I think I prefer the hard way."

"Oh, yes, I think I do, too."

Paying no attention to the jumpy light or the paper man or the shadow that entered Room 212, the angels flipped upside down and began fighting against the buoyancy of their halos, struggling not to spin upright. The one who stayed upside down longest would win the papery dead. The other would take the flickery light, fully aware that size isn't everything; sometimes, the smaller, the feistier.

"Oh, stop, stop, oh, stop," said Leminisse, but the words couldn't halt the push of a halo determined to regain its altitude.

Up the angel turned, and then came Harjo, comforting, "A valiant effort, and well spoken. There's no better four-letter word."

"I like stop. I like it as well as anything."

"I couldn't agree more."

"But I suppose two-letter words have advantages, too. What do you say, shall we go?"

"I don't see why not. I'm as ready as you are."

Leminisse turned to address the light. "It's not difficult for anyone if you go along. We can stop any time you want. Just let us know if you need a little break. Do you happen to like a good rain?"

I like rain better than forests. I like rain if it's city rain.

"I don't know if we can manage that," Leminisse said, motioning the way, "but hold on to that thought. Aren't a rainbow of open umbrellas in a city lovely?"

"Oh, yes," Harjo said, "I agree."

The light, once in motion, twinkled ahead of the procession, the paper man close behind. The angels settled back to coast. It was nicer to coast than to haul on a rope. Their destination was as close or far as the time it took them to get there. The little light seemed willing to lead them.

About the Author:

Suzanne Heagy has previously published short stories, poetry, and creative essays about literature, and also worked as an editor for many years. She currently lives in West Virginia. Her novel, *Love Lets Us Down*, is set in Indianapolis, also known as the "Crossroads of America." Heagy has lived in six different states and stayed in innumerable hotels, some of them with windows that open. She was a professor of English at Fairmont State University.